CW00592093

NEFERTITI'S PRODIGY

By

K. McLeod

Argyll and Bute Libraries

34115 00385534 9

Copyright © 2007 **Kerrie Ross**

All rights reserved by the author. No part of this publication may be reproduced, stored in a retrieval system or transmitted in any form or by any means electronic, mechanical, photocopying, recording or otherwise, without the prior written permission of the author.

Illustration on cover by Kerrie Ross

ISBN 978 0 9559938 0 0

To Kirsteen Douglas

And

Ivor

*When one door closes another opens, so the saying goes.
When one door closes another slams in your face, so the
joke goes.
For Sheryl, however, "that door" was always for someone
else.*

Until she met Nefertiti.

CHAPTER ONE

Sheryl watched the droopy lids of his eyes fill with water, and pulled out a tissue.

'You've have got some arse on you!' he said, dismissing the tissue. 'You are like a ewe at tupping time.' He moved behind her and pressed his fingers into the small of her back. 'There's plenty of meat on you girl.'

Mr. Rugby was the only person who called her 'girl', and he was the only man whose fingers came near her body. She watched as he fumbled his way into the cupboard beneath the stairs and pulled out a bottle of Aberfeldy.

'Your mother has always been a little on the bony side for me,' he muttered into the dark. 'I like someone with a bit of meat on them, something to grab hold of. The problem with your mother,' he continued, 'is she lives on her nerves. It makes her lean and mean.'

'My mother eats like a horse,' said Sheryl.

Mr. Rugby had one final fumble with the bottle before he stumbled over to Sheryl and handed it to her. She eased it open and placed it on the kitchen table.

'And she don't know a good thing when she sees it,' he continued, pouring out the whisky.

Sheryl motioned for him to stop, but he carried on until the glass was full.

'Take that George feller. If you ask me, she isn't going to get any better offers, not in a wheelchair and certainly not the way she drives it.' Sheryl said nothing. She looked at her full glass and tried to remember if it was her third or fourth.

'Now, what you need is something smooth,' he said, staggering off to the stairs again.

Sheryl threw a shovel of coal on the fire, careful not to look in the direction of the mirror above it. It was the sort of mirror best avoided in daylight, and for the past two hours, she had managed it.

Mr. Rugby pulled out a bottle of Royal Brackla. 'The Marilyn Monroe of malts,' he whispered, and dusted it with his sleeve. 'Full bodied, curvaceous and well endowed,' he read off the label, then looked at Sheryl. 'Whatever happened to peaty?'

****

Later on that night, she sat in front of another mirror behind the bar of the Argyll Hotel. Shifty the barman was playing, 'Islands in the Stream'; and Sheryl was working up to a sway.

'Dolly Parton really hits the spot, don't she?' Shifty said with a toothless grin.

Sheryl smiled and continued to sway until she heard Martin's voice.

'Sheryl! Thought it was you, I could hear you from the car park!'

She looked up to see Martin's reflection in the mirror and standing beside him was the reflection of Imogene. Sheryl smiled a lopsided smile then turned to face her ex.

'Sheryl THIS is Imogene,' said Martin. 'Imogene, Sheryl.'

Sheryl stared at Imogene; she had a body that defied gravity and a face that hadn't cracked a smile since Christmas. Sheryl took a long draw from her cigarette and stubbed it out. Dolly Parton had finished and so had her good mood. She watched Martin place his hand on Imogene's stomach and smile a smile she had never seen before.

'I'm going to be a dad,' he said.

****

Sheryl woke up five minutes before the alarm, with the sort of hangover that makes sleep impossible and any lying position worse than the last.

Ten past seven flashed on her clock.

'Sheryl!' boomed Beatrice. 'It's gone seven.'

'I know.'

'What?'

Sheryl rubbed her temples. 'I said I know.'

'I can't hear you,' Beatrice continued, adding a small cough.

Sheryl spied a glass half full of flat beer. She gulped it down; hoping it, along with the rest of what was in her stomach would stay still. Sam, the cat of unknown origin, sauntered up the bed.

'Sheryl, you awake?'

Sheryl looked at the ceiling, wondering where else she could be at seven o'clock in the morning.

'SHERYL?'

Small snapshots from last night flitted into her mind and she groaned. She let out a huge belch, attempted a stretch and then gave up as her head began to spin.

Beatrice eased herself upright and began hunting around for the television remote.

'Sheryl, any chance of a cuppa soon?'

Sheryl rolled onto her back and groaned.

Beatrice flicked on the television with the remote and rewound last night's wrestling tape.

Sheryl eased herself onto the side of the bed, pulled on her tracksuit and then made her way towards the kitchen, the only warm room in the house. Sam sprang off the bed and began charging in and out of her legs like a ferret on speed, as Sheryl expertly walked around it.

She flipped the kettle on, put bread in the toaster and then sat down with her back against the wall, waiting for her stomach to catch up with the morning's movement. *Nothing mattered*, she thought. Nothing but keeping the contents of her stomach down and finding some cat food that didn't stink of fish.

Beatrice watched the wrestling. Two huge men, dressed in colours only a large muscular man could get away with, circled the ring. They wore Lycra so tight that the only one (in the audience) who couldn't see what was underneath was a short-sighted woman in the back row, half asleep.

Beatrice was almost in heaven, if only she had her tea.

Sheryl shuffled into the bedroom. 'God, that's loud!'

One of the wrestlers grabbed a chair from the commentator's table and belted it across the back of his opponent. The chair hit the wrestler's back and he fell on to his stomach with his limbs stretched out like a starfish. The standing wrestler looked around for applause. When none came, he then yelled some abuse at the audience.

'Good night last night?' said Beatrice, noting her daughter's pasty complexion

Sheryl wondered if a cup of tea would be tempting fate. She forced a smile.

'It's about time you went out,' said Beatrice. 'You've been moping around far too long.' She tapped her daughter's knee, trying to appear positive; not easy with a face as comfortable with disappointment as Beatrice's.

'It was Rugby's birthday,' Sheryl ventured. 'And he was looking for company!'

'Ah, the malt whisky,' smirked Beatrice, picking up a piece of toast. She could just picture the bottles lined up in the larder, and Mr. Rugby's shaky hand pulling down one at a time, tenderly wiping the dust from the labels as he read each one out. 'I remember his 65th birthday,' said Beatrice. 'We almost made it to the Knockando. So you seduced poor ole Rugby into a session, did you? How far did you get? I bet half of them didn't even taste any different!'

'I seem to remember a particularly pleasant Laphroaig,' said Sheryl. 'I even helped him to bed. No, my mistake was to carry on to the pub. That's where things get blurred.'

'I gather you met HIM then?'

'And how did you 'gather' that?'

'You staggered in moaning that song that you constantly played after the split.'

'Shifty's song,' muttered Sheryl.

Beatrice swallowed her toast.

'I thought we had a chance. I thought the split was temporary, then I met....' She jumped up from the seat and raced to the toilet.

'That's right, Sheryl, better out than in,' said Beatrice as she turned up the wrestling tape to drown out the sound of retching.

CHAPTER TWO

Sheryl sat in 'The Stables Café' thinking about brandy, raw eggs and other morning-after cures, idly wondering what sort of sick person came up with the idea when she noticed Lindsey, her younger sister, standing by the front door with an "I've got something to tell you, which you are going to hate" look on her face.

'Sheryl's feeling delicate,' yelled Beatrice, with a sympathetic face.

'Oh,' said Lindsey, with the blank look of someone who had never experienced a hangover before. Lindsey was the sort of younger sister no one would want; she had the same metabolism as Beatrice, a rich amiable husband and an easygoing son. Her main problem in life was what to wear to golf, and how to keep her cleaner from leaving. She ordered a hot chocolate with cream and the 'gooiest' cake available, and then looked at her sister. 'So, what you been up to now, then?'

'Feeling a bit rough.'

'Sheryl, I can't remember a morning when you haven't felt rough.'

'Or needed a good puke,' added Beatrice.

'You've had more hangovers than Mum's had carers,' said Lindsey, ignoring Beatrice's sour look.

'Ain't nothin worse than a hangover when your life's crap,' said a waitress, appearing from nowhere. She plonked a hot chocolate down.

'Crap?' said Sheryl, looking at the waitress, who looked like she had nursed a few herself.

6

'When you've got nothing better to do than get pissed.'

Sheryl eyed the waitress, still young enough to "pull" even in a slightly soiled apron. 'I did not get p...'

'Hanging around ole Rugby again?' asked Lindsey.

'I don't hang around....'

'When there is no one but your mum to commiserate with.'

'Cheers, Mum.'

'When the only way to treat yourself,' said Beatrice 'is to get pissed with some old git down the road.'

'I did NOT get pissed ....'

'Mr. Rugby did, by all accounts,' said the waitress, scratching herself. 'Frances was just in; she said he was still in bed - stinking of whisky.'

'What's he playing at, a man his age?' said Edna from the next table. Edna spent every morning in the café with Mavis, and they had both known Rugby all their lives.

'He didn't even want his porridge,' continued the waitress, acknowledging the two women. They nodded in unison.

'What did you do to him?' laughed Lindsey.

'Not a bloody thing, I told you, I went to the....'

'There's no need to shout, Sheryl, or for that matter, wear a face like a smacked arse,' Beatrice added, with a loud voice.

'Frances said...' the waitress continued.

'You know,' continued Beatrice. 'If you just bothered a bit about your appearance, I'm sure you'd feel better.'

Sheryl wondered if the people across the road could hear her.

'Frances said,' added the waitress, 'she was going to sort him out, starting with his so-called "collection".'

7

'Oh,' said Beatrice, remembering why she didn't like Frances.

'And do you know what the old boy said? The only person touching his "collection" was him, and if he wanted to go to bed wrapped in tin foil, he would.'

Beatrice remembered why she liked Rugby so much.

Lindsey nudged her sister. 'You wanna aspirin or a smoke?'

'He said he would kill any damn bugger who was going to argue with that! And then he told her where to shove her porridge!'

'Aye well, he always did have a good imagination,' said Mavis.

'That's Rugby for you,' muttered Edna.

The waitress moved on, leaving a whiff of fried chips behind, reminding Sheryl that she was still hungry. She wondered why she put up with the Saturday morning shopping, why she was sitting there taking all this verbal abuse. And when did drinking with an old man become a crime? She thought about fish and chips, a smoke and enough beer to make her clothes tight.

'You heard from Martin lately?' asked Lindsay.

'Sheryl knows about the baby!' said Beatrice, still in loud mode. Lindsey, to Beatrice's mind was deaf; the truth was that Lindsay had no idea how to listen, or even pretend to.

'But did you hear about the wedding?' asked Lindsey, as she took a gulp of her drink. 'It's supposed to be a big 'DO'!' she muttered through chocolate lips.

'It's not that big a do,' said Beatrice. 'They're holding it at the Argyll! That place has Irn-Bru on tap and karaoke on a Friday night. Their idea of a buffet is a plate of chipolatas, cheese and onion dip, and a packet of crisps. '

'The Argyll's been taken over,' said a voice from the other table.

'They have a new chef, and they don't do chips after seven, only potato wedges.'

'You knew and you never thought to tell me?' said Sheryl.

'It's a rush job,' yelled the waitress from the back of the cafe. 'She don't want to show in her wedding dress.'

'Show?' Beatrice exclaimed. 'She'll be six months gone by then, the only thing she'll be feeling on her honeymoon will be heartburn and the small sensation of piles.'

A chuckle ran through the café.

'They've asked everyone,' said Lindsey. 'Even you.' She slid an invitation card across the table.

The card was black with gold writing, some would say arty-farty. Sheryl ran her fingers along the crimped edges, and wondered how long the aspirin would take to work.

'She made it herself... ' said Lindsey.

'Pretentious crap!' said Beatrice, taking the card off Sheryl. 'Mind you, that doesn't surprise me, Martin always was a prat. I mean any man who has a hyphenated name.'

'SHE MADE IT HERSELF,' Lindsey continued. 'Imogene IS a calligrapher.'

'How wonderful,' said Sheryl. 'He's having a baby with someone who writes like a monk.'

CHAPTER THREE

Beatrice looked at her cards, leant back in her chair and savoured her dram. George was all that was left, and he looked smug. Beatrice aimed her smile at him. She was as familiar with his weather-beaten face as she was with the moves in wrestling, and she knew what was coming next. Beating George was going to be the highlight of the night, and she intended to enjoy every moment.

Frances lit another cigarette. Why did she come? Poker was not her game; she preferred whist nights, but as there was only the three of them tonight from the 'aces high' card club, she was outvoted. She let out a small trail of smoke and thought about the following day. Beatrice would be in The Stables by lunchtime, crashing her wheelchair through the tables as the school children queued by the take away counter. Her usual ploy was to barge to the front of the queue and insist on paying for her 99p tea and cake offer with the winnings. Frances thought about taking the day off. Watching Beatrice count out coppers with a queue behind her was as painful as listening to her Uncle Rugby after he had spent an afternoon exploring his malt collection.

'Play your hand, George,' said Beatrice, draining her glass.

George met her stare.

'I'll raise you!' he said, pushing forward a 2p.

She pushed forward her coin and another, 'I'll see you!'

'Where's Sheryl?' asked Frances, 'Upstairs; or still at Rugby's?'

'She is at her belly dancing class!' said Beatrice.

'Ballet dancing?' said George. 'Isn't she a bit old for that tutu, dying swan stuff?'

'BELLY DANCING!' snapped Beatrice. 'You know, of Arabia!'

George looked blank.

'Sequins, bras, dance of the seven veils?'

'Belly dancing?' laughed Frances. 'I read about that; a dance for fat women. Apparently, they all go over to Egypt and pick up Arabs for sex.'

'How much you had to drink, Frances?'

'It's true; I saw it in the Record.'

Beatrice said nothing; as far as she was concerned, anyone who read The Record like the bible wasn't worth arguing with. Instead, she turned her attention to George; his immaculate moustache was twitching.

'What you smirking at, then?'

George smiled, he had vague memories of exotic dancing during the war, and for a moment he was transported back to those days when he looked pretty good in a uniform. 'Belly dancing, I see, it is a woman's kind of thing; getting over the break-up, what?'

Beatrice pushed another coin into the centre. 'I'll raise you!'

****

Sheryl stood at the back of her class, numbly thinking about Martin and his pulling power. She twirled her hips and followed the elastic flow of her teacher.

'Knees together, Sheryl, this ain't no LAP DANCING class.'

Sheryl sighed. Nefertiti was a pain in the proverbial. She was a skinny woman, the wrong side of fifty-five, which no amount of black eyeliner and good dentures could disguise. She called herself Nefertiti, others in the class called her 'Naff-arse-tetity' or 'the naff one'.

When Sheryl had started the classes, the teacher was a sturdy 25-year-old Greek called Ardennes, and Nefertiti (who was simply known as Janice back then) was just another pupil in the front row.

Ardennes attracted so many members that the class was moved from the small-carpeted playroom in the community centre, to the badminton court. He had a fondness for Lycra, worn tight, with a black sequined scarf tied in a LARGE knot over his groin, making pelvic tilts the high point of the evening.

He also had a job in the Argyll Hotel.

'Belly dancing is a gift from one free spirit to another,' Ardennes would whisper into a student's ear, while placing his hands on her hips. 'Let the drums unleash them.'

Janice had waited for him to whisper in her ear and place his hands on her hips. When he didn't, she stopped eating carbohydrates and got her belly button pierced. And when that didn't work, she informed Shifty, the barman in The Argyll, about Ardennes and his 'free gifts' from one client to another. It was the only time Ardennes was caught performing pelvis tilts with no Lycra.

He left the next day.

Sheryl felt sorry for the young man. Being caught in the act is undignified enough, but when suspended from a slightly dodgy four-poster bedpost, wearing nothing but a union jack g-string and clutching a pair of crutch-less pantaloons between his teeth, dignity didn't come near it.

Sheryl would squirm uncomfortably as the other members of the class mulled over the gory detail of Ardennes's sex life, some wishing it was themselves who had been suspended from a bedpost.

But Sheryl didn't; it was not that long ago she was known as the girl who put sex into Scottish dancing. She knew, because Mr. Rugby had been in the Argyll and read the walls in the gent's toilets.

It was all thanks to Mavis, who ran the post office. Martin owned the post office. He also owned the flat above, which Sheryl lived in. Mavis had walked in on Sheryl's version of Scottish country dancing, and spread it about Lochgilphead that Sheryl was not only doing a line with a married man, but did it suspended in mid-air like some acrobatic prostitute. *The things I did for Martin*, Sheryl thought, *no wonder I'm good at belly dancing.*

'Strictly speaking, this ain't no belly dancing move, but as my Rodger would say, a bit of spice never harmed anyone.'

The class sighed. After two weeks in Turkey, Nefertiti had suddenly become an expert on all things Middle Eastern. She claimed belly dancing worked 'Miracles down below', or her 'Flower of Scotland', as Rodger liked to call it.

'Six weeks of belly dancing, luv, and you'll be able to laugh and stay dry,' said Nefertiti, tilting her padded bra.

Sheryl wondered about her own neglected 'Flower of Scotland', and Martin, and wished she cared less.

George placed his hand on the table. At first, he was confident until he caught the familiar gleam in Beatrice's eye. Plying her with whisky had been an expensive mistake. He had spent the best part of an evening watching his small pile of coins disappear. He knew what was coming next, gloating by Beatrice and more drink; all from his bottle, of course.

He smiled to himself, she was so damn predictable.

Sheryl rode her bike home from class, all the time thinking about sex, or as in her case, the lack of it. It had been ages since she had had any. In fact, she had forgotten what it was like to wake up with a smile on her face and someone warm close by. She stood by the gate of her house, and looked up at her mother's bedroom window. Beatrice was in bed, the television light was flashing through the curtains and Sheryl could hear wrestling. She opened the gate, left her bike by the shed, and walked inside.

'It hardly seems fair,' said Sheryl, trying to shut the bedroom window, she looked at the lock and jiggled it a bit. 'All those years he never wanted a baby, and then SHE comes along...'

'You going to be long with that? Johnston is on soon.'

Sheryl tugged harder on the seized lock, but it refused to budge. 'I've decided I don't need a man,' she said.

'Women usually say that when they haven't had their hole for ages, and there is no hope on the horizon. It makes them feel like they have a choice,' said Beatrice, while watching the TV.

Johnston stood in the centre of the ring. The only thing that covered his six-foot dark frame was a pair of tight leather underpants cut high around his backside.

Sheryl sprayed WD 40 on the lock and gave it a sharp pull.

'You never did like Martin, did you?'

'Well, no mother likes to see her daughter hitch up with a married man; it means he is used to lying!'

'I told you, it was an open relationship.' Sheryl tried the lock again 'It was all above board.' The handle came off in her hand.

Beatrice turned up the volume of the TV. Johnston ran from one side of the ring to the other before climbing onto one of the corner posts and holding his arms in the air. The crowd cheered and began throwing knickers.

Steel Ice entered the ring. He had a tight butt, which he chose to show off in a pair of leopard print leggings. He picked up one of the underpants from the floor, rubbed it under his armpits and tossed it into the audience. The crowd booed.

Steel Ice and Johnston circled the ring. Johnston's back foot slid on a pair of lacy knickers. Steel Ice grabbed his leg and bent it backwards, Johnston put on a good show of pain

'You were still second best.'

'For the love of GOD!' shouted one of the commentators.

Sheryl looked at the handle in her hand then went downstairs to her toolbox.

Steel Ice crashed down on Johnston's leg with his knee. When Steel Ice stood up, Johnston rolled over and slid under the ropes and out of the ring. Steel Ice followed, picked up a chair and ran towards Johnston.

'Where is his wife now?' Beatrice yelled. 'She's in his house, well set up.'

Sheryl stared at her father's box of tools; she picked it up along with her drill and walked back to the bedroom.

'Why did you have to fool around with HIM for? You've got nothing now.'

Sheryl turned on the drill.

'I'll get by somehow,' she yelled over the noise.

'Get by? How will you get by? You were working for 'hands on Martin' remember, not much reference that.'

Sheryl pulled apart the old lock and tossed it in the bin. Her thoughts drifted to Martin.

The first time she had met him was in the Argyll. Martin had just opened an underwear shop called Peek-a-Boo in Lochgilphead, everyone thought he was mad. Lochgilphead was a small town. Small enough to be satisfied with a Co-op the size of newsagents, and an even smaller Spar, how could an underwear shop pay? But Martin had ideas; he wanted to move up in the world and underwear with a difference was the way to go, that and some adult toys.

He walked into the Argyll and saw Sheryl knocking back the whisky, and singing Dolly Parton songs to Shifty. Shifty was trying to shut her up by offering her a cigarette. Martin at the time had a passion for big ballsy women, and Sheryl with a drink in her was ballsy, and big. He sidled up beside her and tapped her on the shoulder. Sheryl, still singing to Dolly Parton, spun around on her stool and skidded onto the floor. Martin was in lust.

'Run my shop for me,' he said, helping her to her feet.

Sheryl looked in to his puffy face and thought, *Why not?*

Those were the days, thought Sheryl, pulling the new lock out of its packet. She started her drill again.

It took Martin a couple of weeks to get past first base with Sheryl, but once she let his small round body into her bed, she was hooked. Martin pressed all the right buttons, and on a good day, he made her laugh. What did she care what her mother or anyone said. Martin made her happy, in the beginning.

But there are only so many ways you can flog a vibrator, and Martin began to look elsewhere to make money. He bought a shop in Oban and turned it into an art gallery. 'Tourism, not sex, is the answer,' he had said, and hired Imogene the calligrapher to run the shop, then Martin went all arty-farty.

The crowd on the TV were cheering louder, baying for Johnston's blood. Steel Ice crashed the chair on Johnston's back, and he fell to the floor; Johnston didn't move.

'What the hell do women see in Martin? I mean, what sort of grown man drives a sports car in Lochgilphead?' said Beatrice.

'HE LIKED intelligent women,' Sheryl muttered, checking the lock one more time and than closing the window.

'He just said that so you wouldn't notice him staring at other women's tits.'

Sheryl looked at the TV; Johnston's beautiful black body was being carried off on a stretcher. 'His new woman has a body that defies gravity!' she said, 'He'll not be looking elsewhere now.'

'The baby will see to that!' snapped Beatrice.

Sheryl said nothing; she had seen his new 'piece', as Beatrice liked to call her, and thought it would take more than a baby to dislodge her assets. She stared at the TV, waiting for Johnston to return.

****

George parked his red Merc by the library ramp and jumped out. He walked around to the back, pulled the wheelchair out of the boot, unfolded it and then wheeled it around to Beatrice's side of the car.

Beatrice glared at George. 'Why do you insist on driving me about?'

George opened the door.

'I mean, I'm not a bad driver, there are only a few dents on the car.'

George motioned Beatrice to slide onto the chair.

Beatrice inched her small bum into the chair, then switched on the controls. George moved behind to push. Beatrice, however, dismissed him with a wave and jolted the chair into first gear. The chair, not sufficiently warmed up, jolted, spluttered, then moved forward. Beatrice rammed it into second gear, then third, by the time the chair had hit the library door, it was in fourth gear and she had made her familiar crash entrance.

'Hi Beatrice,' said Steven, not even looking up from the reception desk.

Beatrice grunted and continued on to the staff room. There were three people in the library that morning, and not one looked up. Not one was surprised as she crashed by in her wheelchair, and all three expertly moved their feet out the way, like they had done a million times before.

'Coffee, Steven? That's if this old crock can manage a hot kettle.' Beatrice paused and looked at the familiar faces now watching her, then crashed her chair through the staff room door and put the kettle on. 'Two years ago, I was a vegetable,' she muttered. 'Couldn't even wipe my own arse.' She looked at the empty coffee jar. 'TEA, STEVEN? They had me for dead; tell me I can't drive.' Beatrice crashed two cups onto the bench.

It had been two years since Beatrice had had her stroke, and she was proud of what she had achieved, she even had her old job back in the library.

'MINT OR NORMAL?' yelled Beatrice.

Steven muttered something about mint.

Beatrice crashed through the staff room doors with a cup

balancing on each arm of the chair. Steven watched the liquid move with the motion of the chair, almost but not quite spilling. 'Or whatever you got,' he said.

Beatrice wheeled herself behind the desk as Steven gingerly lifted the cups from the arms of the chair. She took up her usual place behind the desk, and surveyed the library like a captain at the helm. She liked to think she ran a tight ship and that poor old Steven would be lost without her. She berated the young mothers for making too much noise, and did her best to scare off any children she considered "badly behaved". She dealt with pensioners with an extra loud, "Are you stupid as well as deaf?" voice, and snapped at any students who dared to ask for an unavailable book. And as for those who brought in a late return; they never did it twice.

Steven, who had been working in the library for a year, had still not convinced Beatrice that it was he, and not her, who was the trained librarian and had the final say. He spent his time placating customers not used to Beatrice's gruff ways, and soothing young mothers whose children refused to go near the "Crabbit old lady in the wheelchair".

He also read "How to write a novel" manuals. He was secretly working on a murder-cum-western story, loosely based around a gun slinging redhead, just like Sheryl. He pictured his heroine standing behind some bar, wrapped in taffeta and lace, with a tiny pistol strapped to her thigh. Sheryl had no idea. She just assumed he looked at all women in a peculiar way.

****

Sheryl stood in the middle of the Community Centre badminton room, practising her hips circles, the motion felt good, she closed her eyes and moved to the drums.

'Good, Sheryl,' said Nefertiti. 'You should think about gettin' a costume. Come see me later, I know what works for big ladies.'

Sheryl opened her eyes and looked around the room; there were ten big round bums covered in brightly-coloured coin belts just like hers, and not one of them looked out of place.

****

Beatrice pulled out four DIY books from the shelf, hid them underneath the desk in the reception, and then began to write a list. Frances walked in and placed a 'Beat the Pros at Poker' book on the returns desk. Beatrice looked at it and sniffed. Frances picked up the list and read it.

1. Unblock drain outside kitchen.

2. Replace rowan outside your window.

3. Replace slates next chimney.

If wet -:

1. Fix washing machine <u>AGAIN.</u>

2. Change lock on my bedroom window; <u>THEY DON'T MATCH.</u>

'This is for Sheryl?' asked Frances.

'Uh-huh,' said Beatrice, busy with returns.

'Do you not think she needs pampering?'

'Hard work is what she needs.'

'She's been working for months at your place, and she still looks as miserable as the day Martin dumped her.'

Beatrice threw her a look; she liked to think she knew what was best for her daughter; plenty of hard work and, of course, Mr. Rugby.

Beatrice had a theory, which she would tell to anyone who stood still long enough. 'What a dumped woman needs is the chance to turn down the advances of another man,' she would say, and Mr. Rugby was nothing if not persistent. The fact that he had just had his eightieth birthday and had a hygiene problem meant little to Beatrice.

Others would argue.

'How is a persistent old man sprouting a variety of growths on his face going to cheer Sheryl up?' said Frances. 'She was dumped, she came home to find her possessions stuffed in bin bags, the locks changed and the worst Dear John letter I've ever read. Mr. Rugby's groping is hardly going to take away that pain.'

But Beatrice was adamant.

CHAPTER FOUR

Sheryl left the Community Centre, drove into the main street of Lochgilphead and parked by the Spar. On the passenger seat was a pamphlet Nefertiti had given to her along with everyone else in the class. On the front was a picture of a huge woman dressed in an amazing costume, with the heading:

BELLY DANCING GOES LARGE

Inside was an article about Kelly, the huge woman in the amazing costume.

OUTSIZE KELLY OUTCLASSES THE REST

Being a size 20 doesn't stop our Kelly from pulling in the crowd!

Some of the class members took offence. Sheryl felt inspired.

She pictured herself dressed in Kelly's amazing costume. She pictured herself dancing in front of someone sexy like Johnston. She decided to make herself a costume.

****

Beatrice began to go through the returns pile, underneath lay Steven's notebook, as it fell to the floor, Frances picked it up.

HOW THE WEST WAS WON

BY

STEVEN PIPER

Was written on the front. Frances opened it and the two women, after a small amount of protesting by Beatrice, began to read.

Sheryl was the type of woman hard to forget; a gun-slinging barmaid who made the West a safer place. She held no prisoners. With a tiny pistol strapped to her succulent thigh, and a smile that would melt the proverbial, Sheryl was the DOG'S BOLLOCKS.

Beatrice turned the page....

He took one look at her flowing hair and ample bosom and decided one look was not enough. Lust stirred in his loins. Sheryl was everything he dreamed of and more. She even pulled the perfect pint!

Beatrice looked at Frances, 'I had no idea. I just assumed he looked at all women that way.'

Sheryl worked the bar like a pro. 'Keep 'em coming,' he yelled as he eyed her voluptuous hips. She turned; caught his eye...she knew what he was thinking. 'Skull your whisky, Porter,' she said 'it's your last!' Little did she know that Porter was already on her side!

Steven wandered past the desk and picked up the mail. Beatrice slid his notebook under the shelf, 'Alright then?' she said, with a small cough.

Frances flashed a smile. 'Hi Stevie,' she said sweetly.

****

Sheryl left the main street with a decent pair of scissors for sewing, a handful of cotton reels and a bag of old jewellery from the Bosnia shop. She jumped in the car and drove to the library; maybe they would have some sort of book about belly dancing there. She parked by the ramp and walked into the library, then she remembered it was Friday, fish and chips night.

Every Friday night over a fish supper, Beatrice went over her list of jobs that needed doing around the house. Sometimes, Sheryl wondered if she could ever look at a piece of battered cod again without thinking of drainpipes and handy foam. But tonight was going to be different. Tonight over her fish supper, Sheryl intended to plan her costume.

Without looking at her mother, she walked past the reception desk. Steven looked up.

'Can I help?' he asked.

Sheryl said nothing; she knew where the Middle Eastern section was. She pulled out a couple of volumes of Turkish Embrace, a small book called Eastern Rhythms, and then with the agility of a yoga teacher, she sat on the floor to read.

Beatrice watched her daughter and wondered which charity shop she had got her outfit from.

Steven watched and wondered about offering to help.

The first time he had met Sheryl, she was pushing Beatrice up the library ramp, the chair battery was flat and she was getting the blame. She pushed like a powerhouse with a face he reckoned hadn't smiled, let alone laughed in weeks. From that moment on, he dreamt of making her smile.

Sheryl walked back to the counter and plonked her books on top of the list. This weekend, she was going to do something nice for a change.

Steven studied the books. 'Sheryl's a belly dancer,' Frances told him. He opened Turkish Embrace Volume One and came face to face with a photograph of large pregnant woman circling her bare bump under the sun.

Beatrice pulled the list out and slid it over the woman's bump. Sheryl looked at the list and saw her weekend stretched out before her, and the costume she was hoping to make become just another dream.

'I'm busy this weekend,' she said in a low voice.

Without a word, Beatrice stamped an elderly woman's Patricia Cornwall (in large print).

'I have plans of my own!'

'Plans, what plans?' said Beatrice, thumping her stamp even harder on a Steven King. 'Since when did you have plans at the weekend?'

Sheryl turned to Steven with a pink face. 'Last weekend, she had me unblocking the downstairs loo. She read out the instructions, while I was up to my armpits!'

Steven watched Sheryl with ever-increasing respect, Belly dancing and plumbing. He sighed.

'As I said before,' said Beatrice, 'it's best to keep busy when you're alone!' She pushed the novels towards the elderly woman, who had no intention of moving. 'It's not easy being the wrong side of thirty-five and dumped.'

'I told you,' said Sheryl. 'I have things to do.' She caught the eye of the elderly woman, who looked like she didn't believe her either. Six months of living with a mother who had selective hearing and a permanent "Yeah right," look on her face had left Sheryl feeling that most folk doubted her. She watched her mother reverse her chair into its familiar dent, while Steven expertly moved his feet. Her mother was not going to give up.

Steven felt for Sheryl, he had spent the last year skirting Beatrice's vicious tongue, and was intimate with embarrassment.

'Sheryl, I know better than you what you need!' Beatrice snapped.

Frances turned to Steven, 'you any good at DIY? Sheryl could use a hand.'

Steven thought about Sheryl holding a ladder while he mended something in a manly fashion.

'I told you I have other plans,' said Sheryl.

'Yes, yes, like getting pissed with Mr....'

'I'll do it for you!'

The two women looked at the small frame of Steven. Sheryl wondered if he could lift a ladder.

'I'll do it, I often help my landlady,' he lied, mentally going through his friends for anyone who knew the least bit about drainpipes, plastering or any sort of joiner work.

'You any good at leaks?' Beatrice stared at Steven.

'Oh definitely, leaks are just my thing. Yes, I'm big on leaks, lethal, in fact!'

****

Sheryl stood in the middle of her room looking for a clear space on the floor. She put nothing away. She didn't notice the empty plates with leftovers smeared across them until she stood on one, or the pile of dirty clothes until she ran out. She happily watched the dust settle on everything in clumps, and slept in a crumpled bed; with Sam, and any peculiar smell that either of them chose to make. Sometimes, she was even happy in her room.

When Sheryl had lived in Martin's flat, she was a woman ready and waiting for her lover. A lover who liked things clean, and even as his visits dwindled and the sex evaporated, she still lived, waiting, in a state of sterile agitation.

Until recently, the walls in her room had been a pasty green, with the odd damp patch breaking the monotony. But that was before Sheryl discovered wrestling, and more importantly, Johnston.

She hadn't always liked wrestling; in fact, when she first moved in with her mother, she hated it.

But after a few drinks late at night, wrestling grew on Sheryl. She found herself lingering after helping her mother to bed. In the silence, they watched, and Sheryl grew to appreciate the finer points of a hard black body with more muscles than a seabed.

She tuned Mr. Rugby's television to wrestling on Sky, just so she could watch the highlights while swerving the Hoover across the floor. Mr. Rugby didn't mind, he liked having Sheryl about the place. She didn't nag him when he put a bottle of whisky on the shopping list. She didn't tut when he took one in the afternoon, and she pretended not to notice when he hadn't shaved for a week, or forgotten to put his teeth in. Sometimes, she even joined him in a dram.

Every week, she trotted down to the local newsagents for a copy of the 'Ultimate Wrestling' Magazine (claiming it was for her mother). She bought every back issue with an article on Johnston.

She painted her walls dark blue, then covered them with pictures of Johnston.

There was Johnston in jeans.

Johnston standing with a towel wrapped around his hips and sweat rolling down his smooth skin; looking mean.

Johnston with his arm wrapped around his pint-sized mum, both wearing a Tee shirt with the slogan, "JOHNSTON KING OF THE

RING" splashed across it.

And Johnston flying across the ring with red trousers stretched across his thighs so tight, she could almost see the hairs on his legs.

They all had their appeal, but her new poster was her favourite, and was heading for the precious place of the ceiling. It was full length, and gave an impressive display of Johnston's dark muscular chest, and long hair. Now she would be able lay in her bed and stare to her hearts content at Johnston, and that tiny tattoo around his nipple.

She scrambled across the bedroom clutter, balanced herself with one foot on a cupboard and another on her bed head, and pinned the poster to the ceiling.

****

Beatrice, on the other hand, was downstairs preparing for another game of rugby on TV. She wheeled herself back and forth from the kitchen to the sitting room, carrying nuts and beer and getting in the way of Steven, who was busy assembling his DIY equipment.

Years ago, she had been a successful sportswoman propelling her tiny body into feats of acrobatics, still talked about in some sporting circles. She had been a champion in many amateur clubs, and had a cupboard full of trophies hidden away, which she couldn't bare to look at.

Beatrice switched on the TV and wondered how long it would be before Sheryl would start that awful racket she called music.

****

Sheryl looked in the mirror and shimmied, first her stomach, and then her breasts. It seemed odd after all these years of covering up her body, she was now shaking and swirling it about the place. She pulled her top off and took another swig of wine, then turned her music up.

****

After assembling and reassembling his tools for an hour, Steven decided it was time to go mend what he had promised to mend. Lindsey had come around for a "how are you" visit with her mother. But after watching Steven's fumblings with the ladder, she decided watching him would be better value. She stood at the bottom of the ladder and handed Steven a chisel.

'What kind of noise is that?' asked Steven, checking the ladder was firmly planted on the grass.

'THAT'S Sheryl's belly dancing music,' said Lindsey.

'Oh,' said Steven as he stood poised at the bottom of the ladder, he rattled it a bit then looked up, it wasn't that high. He turned the chisel in his hand. 'Maybe I need something sharper,' he said, trying to appear knowledgeable. He fingered the blunt edges, trying to remember all he had looked up the night before about windowsills and handy foam.

'You don't know what you are doing, do you?' said Lindsey.

'What makes you say that?' Steven replied as casually as possible, while staring up the ladder.

'Cause you're at the wrong window,' she said.

****

Sheryl wrapped a scarf around her hips; and waited for the right beat. She circled her hips, varying the size, all the time watching in the mirror. She had developed a fixation for her belly and was beginning to grow a fondness for the pink flesh, as it rolled to the music.

Sheryl circled her pelvis to the rhythm of the music, and then broke into a shimmy, her favourite move.

Sheryl took to shimmying like other people took to drink; she never knew when to stop. She shimmied in the shower, when vacuuming Mr. Rugby's home, even when standing over a fry pan for her mother. Sheryl could shimmy every part of her body. She shimmied her breasts while driving, her hips while ironing Mr. Rugby's clothes, her bum while cleaning the floor; she just loved the feel of shimmying.

Mr. Rugby spent all his spare time hunting out creased clothes. His main aim in life was to keep the ironing basket full; and his floor dirty; watching Sheryl shimmy was better than Carol Vorderman on Countdown.

Sheryl stood in front of her mirror, marvelling at the obedience of her muscles. She rolled her hips to the melody and flexed her stomach in and out like perfect waves. For once, she was in tune with her body.

****

Steven looked up at Sheryl's window; the hypnotic beat of drums blasted from the closed curtains. He grabbed the bottom of the ladder and shook it a little. He took a few steps.

****

Frances had decided to visit Beatrice as she always did on a Saturday afternoon. She arrived with a poster in one hand, a cigarette in the other and a "just passing, thought you could do with cheering up" look on her face. She slid the poster onto Beatrice's knee, collapsed into her usual chair and inhaled the last of her cigarette. 'You'll have seen this then?' she coughed. Beatrice read the poster.

WRESTLING COMES TO OBAN
LOCK UP YOUR DAUGHTERS
LOCK UP YOUR SONS

CAUSE THE BATTLE OF EPIC PROPORTION HAS ONLY JUST BEGUN

JOHNSTON, STEEL ICE AND MANY MORE WILL BATTLE IT OUT FOR THE KING OF CELTS EXTRAVAGANZA

'I heard Nefertiti's been asked to belly dance at it,' said Frances.

'No.'

'According to Shifty, the Sports for Scotland Committee organised the whole thing, and you know who's on THAT Committee.'

Beatrice stared out of the patio doors; Sheryl's window was just above and Beatrice had a grand view of Steven fumbling with a ladder.

'No?'

'Chubby the butcher, and she has a thing for Nefertiti.'

'That's just cause she calls her darl, and Chubby is too stupid to realise she calls everyone darl,' said Beatrice. She turned down the TV. Lindsey was now offering to help Steven.

'Well, I heard different. According to Shifty, Imogene was in Chubby's and made some remark about mutton, lamb and Nefertiti's inability to fill a padded bra, and Nefertiti was standing right behind her.'

'Oh?'

'Apparently, she told Imogene where to shove her quill and Chubby has been in love ever since.'

Beatrice stared out onto the scruffy lawn. Who the hell was this Nefertiti?

Frances referred to her as 'that game old bird' ever since Nefertiti performed for the Old Folks Christmas dinner in the Stables. 'She didn't just dance,' said Frances. 'She came out of a cake, stripped off her seven veils and handed out free Turkish delights. She put the women off their plum pudding, and inspired the men to dance, one of the old boys had a turn and another pulled his hip out. And it was Nefertiti who did first aid; till the ambulance came.'

Rugby had other names for her, most of which he had read off the wall in the Argyll gents, Menopausal Lap Dancer being his favourite.

Beatrice just knew her as the 'Is Sheryl there, Darl?' voice on the end of the phone, and as the bony woman in the belly dancing poster on the Co-op notice board, who had obviously just been given a new set of dentures.

'So it's her I got to thank,' said Beatrice.

'What for?'

'For Sheryl doing weird thing with her pelvis in her bedroom instead of mending the rowans for me.'

****

Sam was on the roof, looking down at the large jump and then he spied the ladder.

Steven was grimly hanging on to the sides of the ladder. He had managed to ease himself up and was level with Sheryl's window. Her window was opened, but the curtains were closed. Steven didn't see Sam; neither did Lindsey, who instead of holding the ladder was texting. For a moment, Steven hesitated then he took another step, the ladder wobbled, he gripped onto the window ledge and looked up to see Sam on the top rung of the ladder.

'Bugger off,' he whispered.

Sam, who had a fondness for softly-spoken men, moved down a rung.

'Hiya,' yelled Lindsey into her phone.

The curtains blew open and Steven caught a glimpse of Sheryl dancing.

Sheryl caught a glimpse of Steven's face at the window. But it was just a face to her, and she quickly assumed it to be burglar. She slammed the window shut as Steven's soft voice was drowned out by the music.

Frances and Beatrice stared out on to the scruffy lawn; the ladder wobbled a little.

'Lindsey?' yelled Steven.

'You know, Sheryl could do worse,' said Frances. 'He's very clean and he's under fifty.'

A few crumbs of plaster sprinkled to the ground, followed by heavier rubble.

'And willing; how many would fumble up a ladder?'

Sheryl ran into the lounge mumbling something about a burglar, but stopped in her tracks as she recognised the ladder and the ginger blur that was now cascading down the ladder, accompanied by a feline scream.

'Sam!' she yelled.

Then with dignified silence, Steven tumbled past the window. With a dull thud, he landed in the nettle patch and let out a muffled 'Bugger.'

Beatrice reversed her chair to the side cabinet. 'Another dram?' she said. Frances held out her empty glass. Sheryl ran outside.

Steven lay on the ground with nettles artistically arranged about his person, mumbling incoherently.

That morning, he had woken up feeling positive. He had visions of himself coming down the ladder looking like a bit of rough out 'Lady Chatterley's lover'. A little bit of plaster dust, he thought wistfully, could do wonders for his sex appeal. He had pictured himself mending the leak and walking into the kitchen with a few tools slung around his hips, looking like Sean Bean.

'I'm alright, our Sheryl,' he muttered as Sam jumped on his chest, then he closed his eyes.

CHAPTER FIVE

That evening, Steven stayed for supper. It was Frances's idea; she had heard that he was a great cook and if she was staying for dinner, just for a change, she would like something edible.

Steven stood by the sink, his body still throbbing a little. He itched for his Mr. Muscle spray; the kitchen had that slightly greasy look from constant fry-ups and minimal cleaning. He thought about polishing the surfaces, but took one look at Beatrice's idea of a cleaning cloth and gave up on the idea. Instead, he arranged the food on to four plates and put the kettle on.

He whistled a little to himself, looked down at Sam and handed him a small piece of cheese. Thanks to Sam, Steven had spent half an hour under the administering hands of Sheryl. She dabbed his cuts and nettle stings with whatever she had in the cupboard, and placed a few plasters in the appropriate places. None of the creams worked, but he didn't mind.

Sheryl, on Beatrice's insistence, opened a bottle of wine. She poured, then waited for Beatrice to complete what was hopefully her final lap of the kitchen. Steven carried over two plates of seared peppers filled with odd bits from the cupboards. Frances followed behind with two other plates and a look of anticipation on her face.

In the lounge room, the wrestling had just started. Steven walked in on an Aussie duo running into the ring while swinging didgeridoos.

He had never seen wrestling before. He didn't even have a TV. What he had was a small flat, a computer, a stereo, a collection of records that took up the width of his lounge, and a very pleasant landlady who gave him free use of her herb garden for the odd jar of homemade pesto. He had a large blender, a very attractive old pestle and mortar, and a newly bought pasta maker. He liked to cook while planning his novel, and regularly brought titbits for Beatrice to have at work. Eventually, Beatrice had given up taking her lunch as Steven's titbits turned into a full-scale picnic.

'How's the belly dancing?' asked Steven, as he toyed with the idea of bringing over his pasta maker, would that be too forward?

'Great! My teacher says I have an Arabic pelvis!'

The fanfare for Uno Sumo blared from the television, as two small men in blue underpants raced forward waving a Japanese flag. The crowd booed.

'And that's a good thing?' Beatrice looked at her daughter, 'That's why you wrap yourself in those flowing skirts? And pour olive oil on everything?'

'Apparently, the Arabs used to rub olive oil onto their hips,' said Steven, 'They say it's good for the skin.'

The women looked at him.

'I think you will find that it is the perineum,' said Beatrice, reversing herself back to the sink and grabbing the whisky bottle.

'And here he is, hot from England,' yelled a commentator over the blare of Rule Britannia. The crowd cheered as a white knight swirling a sword marched into the ring. Mad Brady, one of the commentators, stood in the ring, while Uno Sumo stood in the corner restrained by his Japanese sidekicks

'So, St Michael, are you ready for the fight of your life?'

The knight removed his helmet, waved to the crowd and then handed his sword to a small woman dressed in a fur-covered bikini. 'I am here to defend the honour of my Lady Ginger, and to thrash the living daylights out of all who have tarnished her name.' Some women sighed in the audience. Uno Sumo almost broke free from his restraints.

'And soon,' said Mad Brady, 'you'll be fighting in your homeland again. Is your fair lady coming with you?' The crowd roared, a few waved Union Jacks. 'That's right, folks, the negotiations are over. The fight for the Celtic Title is on. England will never be the same again!'

'They're coming to England?' said Sheryl, her heart beginning to thump.

'Johnston too,' said Beatrice.

'What! You knew and you never thought to tell me?'

'Yeah, it's bigger than the Olympics!' Mad Brady began to shout, before giving Jim, the other commentator, a friendly thump on the shoulders. Jim looked back with the expression of someone who didn't think thumps on the back were friendly.

'They'll be in Oban next week,' said Frances.

'Your pal, Nefer-whatisname is dancing for them,' added Beatrice.

'What? When?' Sheryl started to pant; Johnston this close. 'We must get some tickets.'

Beatrice pulled the pamphlet from the coal bucket and tossed it across to Sheryl; the first thing Sheryl saw was the words "sold out" in red letters.

About the same time, a taxi pulled up by the gate, tooted loudly and then drove up the drive. No one heard over the TV or saw the two pink legs slide out of the car. She paid the taxi and struggled with her luggage to the front door. When no one answered, she, with her luggage beside her, fumbled around the back and peered into the patio doors.

Beatrice jumped with fright then she caught sight of the dentures.

'And now as East meets West,' Mad Brady yelled into the microphone, 'and Japan's most famous export clashes with the heroic white knight,' he took a breath, 'we're in for a fight of colossal proportions.'

Jim looked at the camera with a blank expression. He was about to say something, but never got the chance as Uno Sumo promptly sat on his opponent.

'Let us in, Sheryl,' said the voice from the patio door, Sheryl opened the door, the pink legs walked in, leaving her luggage for some mystery porter to deal with, and she held her hand out to Beatrice. 'I am Nefertiti, you must be Bea.'

****

Her eyes were red and her mascara a little smudged, but Nefertiti held herself erect, and only after finishing the last of Frances' cigarettes did her story emerge.

'I've left 'im, that Rodger. I told him there are some things private, some things for just us, but would he listen? He says I knew all along, he says it's bleeding art. I call it an .... intrusion.'

She dabbed her eyes and pushed her glass toward the whisky bottle, Sheryl filled it. 'He's been paintin' my Flower of Scotland,' she wailed.

Only Sheryl knew what her Flower of Scotland was, and having just eaten the best meal she had had in ages, Sheryl decided not to spoil it by explaining just exactly what Rodger had painted.

'He is going to put them in a show thanks to that "hands on

Martin".' She let out a sob. 'He is calling it "Unveiling the Flower of Scotland", and there won't be a bloody tartan in sight!'

Beatrice decided the woman was nuts.

CHAPTER SIX

That night, Nefertiti never went to bed. Instead, she lay on the couch and every now and then, let out a sob so loud that Sam jumped, screeched and dug his claws into Sheryl. In the end, Sheryl couldn't take any more and went down to console Nefertiti, or at least shut her up. Beatrice, however, had beaten her to it. With a brandy in one hand and an aspirin in the other, Beatrice was doing her best to console. She gave Nefertiti the aspirin, and then took a sip of brandy.

'What am I gonna do?' said Nefertiti. 'My precious Flower of Scotland. How will I face the wrestlers?'

Beatrice looked at the crumpled heap, she had heard a lot about Nefertiti and none of it resembled what lay before her.

This was a woman who, according to those in the Stables, had rode into Lochgilphead on a red moped with a matching leather outfit, and a set of Egyptian drums suspended from each side. At half past three on a Friday afternoon, Nefertiti, ignoring the Lollipop man, had sailed down the main street, tooting her horn as she swerved to avoid those who dared to cross the road.

'Nefertiti's tough,' muttered Rugby, who had watched it all through the windows of the Argyll, 'as tough as day old pizza and that bloody cheese on top!'

Beatrice looked down on Nefertiti; she didn't look so tough to her.

Nefertiti blew her nose, then handed Beatrice the damp tissue, 'I've made up me mind,' she said. She looked at Sheryl. 'You 'ave to come with me to the wrestlers, Darl. Somehow, when you are nearby, I don't feel so bad. I look at you and think there are worse things that can 'appen to women.'

****

In the early hours of the morning, Sheryl lay in her bed and stared at her poster of Johnston, lit up by the streetlamp. She was too excited to sleep. For months, she had stewed over her hero, drooling over his dark nipples and tight butt. For weeks, she had slept under the images that were splashed across her room. And now finally, she was going to meet him. Perhaps her luck had changed, perhaps now there could be a turning point. She put her hands behind her head and wondered what sort of women Johnston liked.

Beatrice tried to get comfortable in her bed and wriggled what she could of her back against the crinkled sheets. How Sheryl could not make a bed properly was beyond her. She flicked on the sidelight, and then pressed the up button on her bed. Shaking her flask of hot chocolate that was really lukewarm, she poured some and began to plan her trip to Oban.

Sheryl didn't know it yet; but it was just a question of persuasion.

Beatrice pictured herself, wheeling down the aisle straight to the front row, with a view so close she would be able to see the sweat rolling down the wrestlers' bodies.

She was going to yell her head off!

She poured some whisky into her lukewarm hot chocolate, tuned her TV to wrestling replays, turned off her light, and in the dark she imagined herself there, this time without the wheelchair.

The next morning, Steven appeared at the door with a manual under one arm, a bag of exotic groceries in the other and a bottle of

Mr. Muscle swinging from his belt. Steven had come back for more. Beatrice let him in and watched him begin to make coffee, which she knew would taste as good as it smelt.

The night before, Steven had walked home nonplussed by what he had seen. His head hung low as he thought of Sheryl getting all hot and bothered over some American wrestler. How could he, a small librarian with a talent for cooking and writing unpublished novels, win the heart of Sheryl? How could he make her notice him, apart from falling off a ladder? He took a hot chocolate to bed and slept on his thoughts, and the next morning, he knew what he had to do.

'She stayed the night,' said Beatrice. 'She says she's got nowhere to go. She said she wouldn't spend another night in that 'bleeding' Martin's flat after what he and Rodger are planning to do. Just wish I knew what she was talking about.'

Sheryl's head was under the sink; *now is not the time*, she thought, *to explain the 'Flower of Scotland'*.

'I brought a manual,' said Steven. He placed it on the table.

Beatrice hovered about the kitchen. 'Mind you, nothing about that Martin surprises me. Sheryl never was good at picking them. She was married to Alistair for ten years before she found out he was gay.'

Sheryl moved her head and banged it on the sink. She screwed harder on the joint, and wiped away the extra grease. Perhaps she should talk about Nefertiti after all; maybe it would put Beatrice off her breakfast.

Beatrice handed her a wrench. 'Sheryl said he was a new man. New man, my arse. HE had a new man every other month.'

'Steven doesn't want to hear about that stuff, Mother!'

But Steven had heard it all before, about a million times as he sat in the library stamping books and filling in forms. At the mere mention of "The wedding", Beatrice would work herself up into a rant, usually at the disadvantage of whatever book she had in her hand. Steven had lost count of the number of books he had had to discreetly mend, or else reorder.

He looked at Sheryl's round body under the sink, working miracles with the plumbing, and he sighed.

George walked into the kitchen with a bottle of red wine and a box of fancy cakes. He nodded towards the washing machine, which was standing like some rusty has-been in the middle of the floor. 'Playing up again?' he said.

Sheryl tossed an old pipe across the floor.

'Nothing Sheryl can't fix.' Beatrice said, 'What do you want?'

'Frances was telling me about your visitor.'

'Frances and her motor mouth,' snapped Beatrice.

Steven picked up the dead bit of pipe and put it in a bin bag. 'I like her, she means well,' he said.

'Bollocks! Means well is just another word for pain in the arse.'

'What's she done to you?' asked George.

'Well, by now, half the town will know we are housing that Nefertiti for one.'

'And what's wrong with that?'

Sheryl tossed another pipe across the floor, this time a little closer to Beatrice.

'And she keeps rabbiting on about some Flower of Scotland art show, which I don't understand, 'cept that Martin's involved, which has to be bad news.'

'Was there much in the washing machine?' asked Steven to Sheryl.

'Just Sheryl's underwear,' said Beatrice, with an extra loud voice, she watched Steven blush, then reversed her chair across the room, just missing George's feet. 'And she wanting Sheryl's to go with her to the wrestling.'

Ah, so that's what's eating her, thought George, he watched Beatrice complete another lap of the kitchen. He had met many women in his time, but none as transparent as Beatrice. 'Did she not ask you to come then?' he said.

'As if I would want to go with that bony woman,' snapped Beatrice.

Sheryl eased herself up from the sink and stretched her solid back. Steven watched, mesmerized by her powerful frame. *What she needs* he thought, *is some luxury, something to make her smile*; he took out some extra dark chocolate from his grocery bag. *Sheryl's coffee is going to be the dog's bollocks*, he thought. It was going to be everything a coffee should be: rich, strong, with just a hint of something more. All he needed now was some milk, which wasn't on the turn, feeling positive, he opened the fridge.

Nefertiti appeared from the lounge room wearing a turban, sunglasses, and an, "I am here" look. She leant against the doorframe and waited for some attention, when none came she spoke. 'My head is thumpin' any chance of a coffee, Darl?'

George and Beatrice continued to stare at the washing machine. 'It's had it,' said George. 'It's over ten years old, not like it owes you anything.'

Nefertiti looked at George. Amongst those in the Aces High club, he was known as the Howard Keel of Lochgilphead. George was a well-preserved man in his seventies, who, to quote Frances, "more than scrubbed up well". Nefertiti thought he had the look of a man of comfortable means, a man who had seen a bit in his time, and yet still knew how to use a Hoover, she knew because she had seen his Merc. *What a pity*, she thought, *that I'm not into older men.*

'Why don't you just give it a good bash,' snapped Beatrice. 'That's what I do!' She pulled a rolling pin from the drawer and gave the side of a machine a few good clouts, and then twiddled with a knob. When nothing happened, she tutted and gave it another thump. The two men looked at her as a loud clatter came from inside the machine.

'Coffee? I thought I smelt some,' said Nefertiti.

'Well if wasn't broken before, it is now,' said George.

Beatrice glared at him then reversed her chair, George swiftly moved his feet. Nefertiti didn't till it was too late. She rubbed her foot and took what she thought was a safe seat.

'You could always get a new one?' said Steven, admiring George's nimble foot action.

'Beatrice splash out and buy a new one?' George arched his eyebrows. 'Old skinflint, with the purse full of moths?'

'I am not a skinflint.'

'Aye right; when was the last time you bought something new?' said George.

'Is there any coffee going?' asked Nefertiti.

'You got the lawn mower out of the skip; sorry, you forced Sheryl to climb into a skip and pull out the lawn mower, which vibrated so much, it left Sheryl with the symptoms of Parkinson for days.'

Steven looked up from the fridge. 'Sheryl was in a skip?' he sighed.

'And what's wrong with that? I've been known to rummage a bit in my time, scale the tip; you never know what you might find!' said Beatrice, looking down at her twisted foot.

Steven lifted out some cream and sniffed it as a mental image of Sheryl in rubber boots scaling the heights of the tip crossed his mind. He decided to whip the cream.

'That's it,' said Sheryl. 'All done.' She began to push the washing machine back into place, Steven jumped to help. Once in place, Sheryl lifted one of the corners up and motioned Steven to place a block of wood under it.

Nefertiti watched Sheryl, inspired.

'Sheryl, you are a REAL Godsend. What you don't have in looks, you surely make up for in brawn. Why, you're almost a man, is there anything you can't fix?'

Beatrice reversed her chair past Nefertiti's seat, and Nefertiti winced.

****

Martin was tired. It had been a hard day; he walked into the bedroom, switched off the light, slid into bed and nudged Imogene.

'She's left him; moved in with Sheryl of all people!'

'Who?' sighed Imogene.

Martin switched on his bed lamp. 'Rodger's muse, his model, the Denture Lady.'

'He should be so lucky.'

'Lucky? That's the show down the pan; Rodger's pulling out, he says he gonna burn every damn fanny ...'

'I told you not to pay for the framing.'

'We need a plan,' he mumbled, his thoughts going to Sheryl. 'She's a good sort; maybe she could persuade the Denture Lady?'

Martin looked at Imogene; he stretched his hand across her stomach and slid down her neat bump. Imogene burped and rolled over onto her back, her face turned pale. 'Oh God,' she blurted, then with her hand over her mouth, she ran to the toilet.

Martin stared at the ceiling. How long did morning sickness last for?

****

No one noticed when he appeared on the drive, not even Sheryl, who at the time, had her head in the boot of the car, collecting tools for her next DIY job. Beatrice had grand ideas of a fire in her bedroom, and it was up to Sheryl to unblock the fireplace.

'How are you?' he said.

Sheryl jumped, knocked her head on the boot then spied the highly polished shoes. She guessed years of sneaking about had given him the ability to walk on gravel silently.

Steven was still in the kitchen working on a light Middle Eastern brunch for Sheryl and the others, when he looked up from his chopping board and noticed a man on the drive. 'Is that Martin?' he said. Beatrice, with the look of smelling something rancid, nodded.

'A bit short, isn't he?'

'HE maintains he is five-foot-eight,' said Beatrice. 'My arse, more like five-foot-five, from where Sheryl is standing, she has an excellent view of his bald patch!'

It was the first time Steven had clapped eyes on Martin 'the gorgeous' as Beatrice liked to put it, and wondered what all the fuss was about. He had seen better bodies in the old folk's home where he delivered library books. Martin had the beginnings of a paunch, which no expensive outfit could hide, and he was short; what decent stud was short?

'I wonder what he wants?' said George.

'Flower of Scotland,' mumbled Steven.

'For God's sake, don't mention THAT when she comes down, I don't think I could stand another session,' said Beatrice.

But it was too late. Nefertiti was already standing in the doorway in her familiar pose, dressed in colours even fluorescent wouldn't describe. She drew herself up to her full height and moved to the window.

'I see 'im,' she said quietly.

'Where's your precious BMW?' Sheryl said, pulling out her drill box.

'It's parked out of sight.'

Sheryl sighed. 'Out of sight' was one of his favourite sayings.

'I have to see you again, somewhere,' he looked around, 'private?'

Sheryl shifted uncomfortably. Maybe he missed her? She took a deep breath and looked into his grey eyes; he crinkled them into a smile. Should she care?

'What do we need to talk about?'

'What about some evening, we could meet?' He stood closer.

She noticed a few beads of sweat on his forehead, and for a moment thought about brushing them away. Instead, she walked around to the side of the car and pulled out a box of nails, a packet of Polyfilla, two small planks of wood and a couple of bags of shopping.

'He looks older than I imagined,' said Steven.

Beatrice snorted, 'That's high living for you.'

'High living and a good-looking mate half your age, that'll kill any man; not enough stamina,' said Nefertiti, putting an espresso to her lips.

'That piece isn't good-looking, she's just blond, and skinny,' said Beatrice. 'My Sheryl's worth twice of her! Nothing a little blue eye shadow and a decent bra wouldn't fix!'

'Hmm, she's very robust, I'll give you that,' said Nefertiti.

Steven never heard. He was too busy watching Sheryl. How could this man not appreciate and cherish the finer qualities of Sheryl, how could he toss her aside then pick her up like a bored child with a pile of toys.? Steven looked at him: no wonder she found Johnston attractive.

Sheryl knew Beatrice was watching, she knew Beatrice was waiting for her to do what she always imagined herself to do; stand up to Martin.

In her dreams, she pictured herself never wanting his attention again, she pictured herself cool and collect, distant and reserved, not slightly flustered, almost flattered by his attention. She thought she had a grip on her feelings, but now faced with the man that had caused her more misery than she had known in a long time, her heart raced just a little. She was confused. It wasn't lust she felt or love, was it emptiness, boredom? Was he the only man that would ever want to see her naked?

Steven walked out into the sun, his feet crunching on the gravel.

He pictured himself as the great Porter in his novel, with a gun slung on his side, tight black jeans and a mean grimace on his face, just as Porter would wear.

'You want a hand with anything?' he said to Sheryl.

'So you're Steven then,' Martin said. 'Lindsey told me about you! Didn't take long.'

'Lindsey? When were you and Lindsey speaking?' asked Sheryl.

'What?' Steven said, trying to sound gruff.

Martin smiled. 'I heard you had an accident with a ladder.'

'And when did you see Lindsey?' interrupted Sheryl. 'Come to think of it, why was she talking to you?'

'We go to the same club!'

'You play golf?' said Sheryl.

'Imogene introduced me too it, she said it would be good for my back!'

'And what would a calligrapher know about back problems?'

'I have proposition for you.'

Martin and his propositions, thought Sheryl. There had been so many.

'What does she see in him?' said Beatrice.

George looked at the squat man; Martin did have a certain charm and he had big ideas, some of which came off.

When Martin first bought 'Peek-a-Boo' the underwear shop, he had little idea of what to do with it, until he saw Sheryl. He figured Sheryl's assets were the best advert for his business, and dressed her up in the best underwear he supplied, and for a while she blossomed. Truth was, after years of living with a gay man, Martin swept Sheryl off her feet with great sex, great laughing, great underwear and an okay job. At least she could call herself a manager.

George, a man of the world had met many 'Martins' in his time. He knew her happiness wouldn't last and he also knew warning her would make little difference.

'Problem is,' said George, 'a ruthless man in business makes a woman feel safe, till he turns on her.'

Beatrice said nothing; she looked out of the window at her daughter. *Poor cow*, she thought.

'Steven looks cross,' said Nefertiti.

'I've never seen him cross before,' said Beatrice. 'The most I've seen is a red face when one of the students plays a prank with a National Geographic magazine.'

Nefertiti and George looked at Beatrice.

'Oh you know, one of those magazines full of black breasts and penises wrapped in bark!'

'Oh,' sighed Nefertiti.

'Oh,' said George with a small cough; he looked out of the window. 'Now what is he doing?'

Porter, thought Beatrice.

Martin pushed his finger into Steven's chest, Steven pushed them away.

'Are they having words?' said Beatrice, 'Over my daughter?'

George looked across at Beatrice and thought he detected a smile.

Sam, who considered the drive as part of his territory, had a high intolerance for visitors in suits (thanks to an unpleasant experience with a persistent insurance salesman), and a keen sense of Sheryl's stress level. He strolled over to Martin and hissed a bit. As no one took any notice, he stretched his legs onto Martin's suit and pressed his claws in.

Martin yelled at Sam, who then gave his other leg the scratchboard treatment. Steven, who by now was on good terms with Sam, picked him up just before Martin gave a kick. Sam, not too keen on being so close to a flying foot, jumped from Steven's arms onto Martin with a hiss, then scrambled about his shoulders for a bit before making a run for it up a nearby tree.

'I never thought much of that cat till now,' said Beatrice.

Martin pushed Steven in the chest; Steven pushed back surprised by his force.

'Should we go out…break it up?' said George.

Sheryl, not quite sure what to do, stood in the middle in an attempt to placate things, but Martin pushed her aside. Steven, fed up with Martin's cavalier approach to his muse and her cat, took a dive at Martin's arm, but only caught his sleeve. Martin tried to pull away, instead he spun around as Steven clung on to his suit, and a ripping noise followed. His polished shoes clipped across the gravel, making an undignified sound as Steven swung him harder and then let go. Martin staggered to his feet and looked down at his sleeve.

'That's my best suit, you arsehole,' he yelled. 'What the hell are you playing at? It's only a cat.'

'Not much of a suit,' Steven puffed. 'Rips like tissue paper!'

'I'll send you the bill, shall I?' snapped Martin, pulling his arm away; he looked down at the large tear with his white shirt poking though. 'It will cost more than you could earn in a week, how much is it now for an overdue book?'

'You ever been in a library?'

'You ever had a real girlfriend?'

'Shut up!'

'Toy fucking boy!'

Steven snapped and swung a punch at Martin. Martin jolted his head away from Steven's fist, lost his footing and fell. Steven, assuming his arm would make contact with Martin's face, overbalanced and landed on top of Martin.

Sheryl looked up at Nefertiti, George and Beatrice beating a trail down the path.

The two men proceeded to roll onto the bags of shopping, tomatoes rolled from underneath and squashed onto Martin's suit, eggs cracked on to the side of Steven's face spreading yolk across his cheek. Sam, spying a bit of haddock, pounced and dragged it from the pile with his mouth.

Memories of wrestling now flashed into Steven's mind, he saw pictures of Steel doing a headlock on Johnston, he saw Steel's body flying through the air and landing on Johnston's. He could hear the crowd cheer; he pulled himself away from Martin with thoughts of a really smart wrestling move, when Sam still with a bit of fish in his mouth jumped onto Martin's face.

Martin swore and screamed.

Sam dropped the fish on Martin's chin, hissed and wrapped

himself across Martin's head.

Beatrice looked down at the ball of fluff and made a mental note to buy salmon from the fishmonger next week.

Sheryl pulled the cat off as Martin glared from one person to the next, his red face already puffed and scratched; he spat out a few strands of haddock from his mouth and swore again.

'So what's all this then?' said Beatrice.

'He started it,' muttered Martin, wiping his chin.

'You started it you mean, you with your stupid suit... Sheryl is too good for you!'

Martin pushed his chest into Steven, who pushed him back with his hands. Martin stumbled a bit and then pushed Steven.

'Wanker!'

'Prat!'

'Tosser...'

Martin huffed some more, looked about at the three women and then pulled a couple bits of tomato from his sleeve, and with a dramatic gesture, slung them at Steven's feet before marching to his 'out of sight' car.

Steven wiped his brow and looked at Sheryl with his chest heaving. Sheryl lent over and picked a few bits of eggshell from his cheek, while Beatrice began to rummage through the scattered shopping.

'Can you do anything with this?' she said, pulling out two mangled mangoes and a flattened sponge.

Nefertiti was inspired. 'I like a man who knows how to handle 'imself,' she said. 'We could use a man like you, couldn't we, Sheryl?'

'What?'

'Come with me to Oban and keep that sodding Rodger and Martin off my back.'

Steven lifted the remains of tomato from his shirt and thought for a moment. 'I don't see why not.'

Beatrice reversed her chair past Nefertiti. This time, Nefertiti was quick on her feet.

CHAPTER SEVEN

While Sheryl was picking through the shopping on her drive, Conway, still in his candlewick pyjamas, was frying up a bit of bacon and black pudding.

Conway was a man who never forgot, a man who clung onto a grudge like a drowning man with plank of wood. A man so eaten up with anger from the past that he no longer made sense. He lived on Rennies, black coffee and meat, which stirred around in his innards like a bullet in motion with nowhere to go.

That morning, his bullet was working overtime. That morning, as he opened up The Argyll Advertiser, he saw something that would make him shake.

NEFERTITI TAKES ON THE BIG BOYS

Our Local Middle Eastern connection will hit the big time next week as she shimmies for the American Wrestlers. 'It was all my Rodger's idea,' says Nefertiti. But everyone knows Nefertiti's talents are as legendary as Egypt itself, and next week, the boys in town won't know what hit them as she performs her new Death by Seven Veils dance to the crowd. 'It's a new piece,' says Nefertiti, 'based on an old Egyptian legend about a mummification that went horribly wrong.'

Beside the article was a picture of Nefertiti posing outside the Argyll. In the background stood a small man with a heavy moustache and sideburns, a man who had never really left the seventies, a man, (unlike most of his contemporaries) who was blessed with a full head of hair and a great set of teeth, which he chose to show off with the aid of Grecian 2000 and a smile that Conway would notice even in a dim bar.

Rodger was not aware that he was in the photo; Rodger had been in the Argyll all afternoon with Martin, making plans about how they were going to take on the art world. His smile was induced by an afternoon of larger and the promise of a prosperous future with Martin. To Rodger, Conway was just a bad memory from a past he would rather forget, a past that he had hoped his Grecian 2000 and new accent would protect him from.

Conway emptied his fridge and threw all the contents into the fry pan, buttered some bread and wrote a note to his wife. He pulled a pile of files and floppies from under his bed and put them into a box, along with a photograph of himself twenty years ago and one of his pet dog, Pep, standing in front of the Azaleas, blocking any view of his wife Edna. He wrote a letter to Archibald McConical, his boss, explaining the need for absence due to unforeseeable circumstances and; forgetting the note, left a message to Edna on their phone about an important mission and don't wait up; for the foreseeable future.

Then with his trusty laptop, he sped off in his yellow Fiesta and headed for the M9.

He stopped at a service station, stocked up on a supply of Rennies and then, remembering Archibald McConical's last words about the need for redundancies, left an abusive message on his phone, finishing along the lines of 'the Omega file is mine'.

'Let's see who's smart now,' he mumbled, while crunching on some Rennies. He tuned the radio up a notch, licked the foam from his lips and headed for the Argyll in Lochgilphead.

****

Every week, Chubby sent the Argyll Advertiser to her half-brother Conway. She wrote a small column in the 'oot and aboot' section, and Conway was her biggest fan.

Chubby saw herself as a woman of wit and intelligence, a woman whose talents stretched far beyond the realms of butchering a cow. Hector, the editor, saw her as a cheap source of local news and was happy to exploit her. Chubby knew more local people than anyone in the area, and her butchering skills attracted more customers than the Co-op on Christmas Eve, selling almost out of date B.O.G Offs. Since Chubby started writing, Hector's sales had doubled, and he was more than happy to indulge in her fantasy of being Lochgilphead's answer to Oscar Wilde.

Every Saturday morning, Conway read out Cubby's Column to Edna, occasionally snorting a small spray of black pudding when he came across something funny. Edna never laughed, but with a tight lip, brushed off the spray from the table and walked from the room. 'She's a lesbian built like a brick shithouse,' she said, 'and she ain't funny.' But Conway never listened, in his dismal world of thieves and ambitious police, Cubby's column was the highlight of the week.

CHAPTER EIGHT

Sheryl is wearing Kelly's glamorous costume and she looks fantastic.
She is standing in the corner of a very posh expensive hotel room;
which is big enough to hold several of her favourite wrestlers, various
people whom she wants to make jealous, and her mother gagged and
bound. In the middle of the floor stands a white piano, behind which is
a small Egyptian band with Hossam Ramzy on the tabla. In this, as in
all her fantasies, Sheryl is slim with a firm butt and a stomach so tight,
you could bounce a penny of it...
Two wrestlers lift her up under her arms as she manages a graceful
pose (similar to that of Ginger Rogers in an old musical) and places
her on the white piano. Sheryl poses as her red hair tumbles down like
something out of a shampoo ad.
Everyone is waiting for her to start.
She begins with a couple of hip flicks and a twist before sliding onto
her knees and performing a back-bend.
The wrestlers applaud, cheering her on, she looks around and catches
Johnston's eye. He is standing close, so close she can feel his breath.
She shimmies then comes up from her back-bend and rolls off the
piano into the arms of...

'Sheryl,' yelled Nefertiti.

Sheryl opened her eyes to a small round of applause from the class, the tail end of a drum solo on a Hossam Ramzy's CD, and Nefertiti looking a little pissed. Sheryl had been lost in the beat of the drums and her favourite fantasy and the only person not impressed

Kerrie McLeod

with her dancing was Nefertiti.

'ARIGHT THEN, let's see some pelvic tilts,' Nefertiti said, and changed the CD.

Outside the Community Centre stood Rodger, in his sharpest corduroy suit; he had a chair in one hand and a bunch of roses in the other. He was looking about to see which window was the right one.

'Let the energy flow from your Flower of Scotland...' Nefertiti said.

Rodger lent the chair against the stone wall and jumped onto it. Through the window, he could see his Nefertiti.

'Your Flower of Scotland is a temple...' she said. 'Which you must cherish...'

The class looked at the window as a dark shadow of a man appeared behind the smoky glass. They watched the shadow push the window open a few inches, slide a single red rose through the crack and wave it in a tantalising manner.

'Nefertiti,' the shadow yelled, with a Birmingham accent.

Nefertiti looked at the window, 'Never let anyone ramshackle that temple,' she continued.

'I wuv you,' he said.

Nefertiti, tight-lipped, walked to the window. Rodger pulled his arm out just in time before she shut the window, clipping the red rose from it stem. Nefertiti picked up the rose head, and with as much drama as possible, tossed it into the bin.

Rodger was a desperate man; a man who had spent most of the morning ignoring all of Martin's 'treat em mean keep em keen' advice. He stood outside the Community Centre with the winter sun beating down on his olive green jacket. Ignoring the caretaker and a

60

few onlookers, he put his chair beneath another window, and with a deep breath, stood on it.

'I wuv yooooou!' he said through the glass, and began to push open the window.

Nefertiti watched the crack at the bottom of the window widen. He was not going to give up; well, she had faced a lot more than him in her time.

She had spent forty years saying yes to a husband called Pete Cleaves. When he died, she ran and never looked back. Instead, she grabbed Ardennes's mantel, not only with both hands, but with a firm pair of taut thighs, and she worked her socks off performing for anyone that asked. She had done every sort of group you could imagine, she had performed in front of the pipe band, brass band, Choral singers, even the young Scottish dancers, who at first were intrigued with the thought of a belly dancer. She had arrived at venues where they took one look at her and forgot the booking. She had even walked onto stages where the audience had continued to talk. But she ignored them all, armed with her sequinned padded bra, and Boot's spray-on suntan, she was the business.

'She's a game old bird!' said many, others claimed it was the wacky backy.

Game or not, this old bird was not for the plucking; there were plenty more dances in her yet, and every morning when she looked in the mirror, she told herself just exactly that.

Rodger thrust another rose through the crack and tossed it on to the floor.

'I still wuv yooooou,' he said. And then he squeezed a whole bunch of flowers through the window and dangled them. A few of the woman giggled. Sheryl was impressed.

'My bugle is lost without his little Nefertiti,' he whispered.

Nefertiti adjusted her coin belt, pulled a tambourine from her bag and walked over to the hand.

'Your bugle will be playing solo from now on,' she snapped. This time, Rodger's jewelled fingers weren't quick enough.

****

Imogene was sitting in Martin's flat, wrapping bandages around Rodger's fingers while thinking about the good old days, when she could keep more than a Jacobs Cracker down without throwing up. Martin was staring at the black screen of the TV while twirling a glass of gin and tonic in his hand.

'We have to get this Nefertiti onside,' he muttered. Sheryl was his only hope. He skulled his gin and tonic, slipped on one of his causal polo neck jumpers, checked himself in the mirror and headed for the Argyll.

****

Beatrice also headed for the Argyll. Tonight was her last night, her last chance to hitch a ride with Sheryl and that damn woman. She had been hatching a plan all morning in the library, a plan that involved a lot of drink and even more manipulation. And she had Lindsey on her side.

Lindsey had watched Beatrice try to live on her own after Robert, Beatrice's husband, had died. Lindsey had watched Beatrice struggle to live an independent life while trying to maintain some sort of dignity, in the face of a wheelchair, a wonky foot and a bladder that refused to hold more than a teacup of pee. And Lindsey had born the brunt of Beatrice's frustration.

While Sheryl was living the good life in Glasgow, Lindsey was dealing with Beatrice in hospital, who spent most of her time complaining through a lopsided mouth and very determined drool.

While Sheryl was exploring a new life in the arms of Martin, while managing 'Peek-a-Boo', she, Lindsey was watching her mother go through more carers than underpants, and driving most of her friends away.

So when Lindsey heard from a neighbour that her sister was sitting outside her flat amongst a collection of garbage bags, looking dazed, Lindsey could have almost kissed Martin. Lindsey was around within minutes and took Sheryl plus garbage bags back to Beatrice.

Beatrice, who was in the middle of an argument with yet another carer about the health benefits of a dram in the afternoon, didn't even acknowledge her daughter, who mumbled something about Martin redecorating the flat and humped her bags up the poky stairs to her old room.

It was her turn now, thought Lindsey.

So come hell or high water, Beatrice was going with Sheryl, no matter how much Sheryl protested; besides, Beatrice's plan may just work.

****

Sometimes on a busy night, Steven worked in the Argyll as an assistant cook. That Friday night, Steven was working on a Prawn Thai curry when Sheryl, with some of the class members, walked into the Argyll. By the time he was serving it to a pleasantly surprised customer, the belly dancers were on their second round, and feeling amicable.

'Hi Steven,' yelled some from the class, Sheryl waved, she was feeling good. She had spent all week polishing off jobs for her mother and then worked like a demon to make a costume just in case there was a chance Nefertiti would let her dance.

'Oban and the wrestlers tomorrow, you think Rodger will be there with another bunch of roses?' asked Kay.

Kay was one of the original members of the class. She was a strong looking woman with grown up children she never talked about, an ex-husband she never spoke of, and a tiny elderly lover who she talked so much about that folk found it hard to look him straight in the eye.

Sheryl took a sip of her whisky and tried to explain the whole Rodger thing.

'Frances says it was Imogene's idea,' added Shifty. 'She says Imogene has this thing about art reflecting the ugly truth of rebirth.'

'Scotland ain't ready for a rebirth,' said Mavis, pushing a vodka and coke towards Kay. Mavis was another member of the class; she took up belly dancing hoping it would change her round, ball-like figure into something a man would find attractive. She had heard about the men in Egypt, and one day she hoped to go there herself (hopefully with her new figure) and see if the rumours were true.

'Nefertiti,' said Shifty, 'sees it as her mission to enlighten.'

'Enlighten what for fuck's sake?' said Mavis. 'It's not enlightenment I need.'

'She's some piece!' said Kay. 'I'll give her that. I wouldn't want to shimmy in front a group of twenty-somethings, no matter how many joints I'd smoked.'

'That Nefertiti would dance for anyone,' muttered Mavis.

Duncan drained his glass, wiped the froth from his mouth and pushed it towards Shifty. 'I'd give her one,' he said. Duncan was a local who spent most nights on the same stool drinking the same drink, and he knew everyone.

'And she's not even that good, not like you,' said Kay pointing her vodka at Sheryl.

'Aye well that's true,' nodded Duncan.

'And what would you know?' said Shifty.

'Ole Rugby,' said Duncan, tapping the side of his nose. 'He's seen her dance; he says it's a work of art watching her Hoover and shimmy at the same time.'

'Aye, but is she enlightened?'

A chuckle ran through the women. 'Like Rodger, you mean.'

'Enlightened or not.' Duncan looked at Sheryl. 'I'd give you one… Just you say the word, luv, and I'd be happy to oblige.'

Everyone now laughed except Sheryl. Shifty offered her a roll up and threw her a wink. She slid the fag between her lips, Shifty lit it and she inhaled. *Always the old gits,* she thought, *always the old guys.*

'Twenty years ago,' continued Duncan, 'I'd have given you a run for your money! So I would!'

Sheryl took another puff of her cigarette while Shifty changed the CD to Dolly Parton, one of Sheryl's favourites. 'Turn it up,' she yelled. Then she noticed Martin walking through the door.

****

Martin had bided his time, he figured that it would take three rounds for Sheryl to be amicable. He walked in at ten o'clock, with his best smile, and struck a casual pose by the bar. He did not want to meet any of the belly-dancing troupe; en masse, these dancing women were scarier than Beatrice after her medical bottle of whisky, and completely resistant to his manly charms. In fact, very few women over the age of twenty-five yielded to his charms these days. Imogene had yielded to his charms and now she spent most of her time in the toilet or looking at catalogues. He sighed, no one could understand the needs of a man like a plain woman...

He watched Sheryl stumble a bit as she walked by.

'Drink, Sheryl?' he said, trying to appear casual like he hadn't been waiting for her for the last hour, but was just passing by; on a whim.

Sheryl looked around for Imogene.

'Whisky; make it a double!' he said.

Sheryl eyed his face, still a little puffy from Sam's attack.

'I've been thinking about everything,' he said.

'Oh!'

'I would like to make 'things' up to you.'

Sheryl stared ahead; Martin's idea of making up for things was sketchy. Most of the time, he had no idea what he was making up for, it was usually that he had not seen her for a while and missed things.

The belly dancers giggled in the distance.

'What are you on about?' she said.

'I need some assistance.'

'An assistant? What about Imogene?'

'ASSISTANCE; besides Imogene and Nefertiti don't quite get on.'

'Oh!'

Martin told Sheryl about Rodger's art show, and his threats to burn every fanny. Sheryl let out a loud laugh; Martin's ideas, they never really changed.

'I'd be grateful, very grateful,' he said.

'And what about Imogene, would she be GRATEFUL?'

'She doesn't need to know, does she? Can we not be adults about this?'

'Adult, is that what Imogene calls it?'

'Imogene has met you in the pub remember, she doesn't really see you as a threat.'

'What!'

'Put it this way, she found our box of toys, and she never connected them to you and me, she just thought I had a very weird nephew.'

Sheryl watched Duncan stagger to the toilet and crash the door shut as his voice echoed a song, and she thought about Martin. He was a man who liked surprises and fantasies, and she, in the past, had taken up that gauntlet with relish.

At first, Martin spent all his spare time at the flat, he was as eager and as much in lust with her as she was in love with him, and for a while it was the best. Even his wife (despite what others thought or said) seemed to think so. 'Thank goodness he found you,' she said one morning when they had bumped into each other at the front of the Co-op. 'I have a tender back myself, in fact, before I met you I had season tickets at the chiropractor.' She was a small woman, a lot older than Martin, still with traces of a great beauty hidden beneath a nervous twitch and thick glasses. As Sheryl clattered away with her trolley for a moment, she wondered if what she just saw was the result of twenty years of marriage to 'hands on Martin'.

'Rubbish,' Beatrice had said, 'that woman was always built like a bird.'

Sheryl, however, was built like an Amazon; she had the back of a miner, the arms of a bricklayer and solid breasts that mesmerized Martin with a life of their own.

'Way hay hay…. Sheryl,' yelled Duncan while adjusting himself.

'Come on, Duncan,' yelled Mavis. 'Keep that belly of yours where it belongs.'

'Way hay hay, Kay!'

Martin ran his finger down Sheryl's arm, she didn't move. 'Islands in the stream, that is what we are,' sang Dolly in the background. Sheryl swayed and let Martin, along with Dolly, toy with her emotions; it had been a long time.

'If you could just talk to Nefertiti, get her to see sense, I'd be so grateful!

Did Martin really want her again? Sheryl needed to think.

She had not been with many men before Martin. There was Alistair, her husband, whose idea of passion was extra chocolate in their cocoa and watching reruns of Dallas. And there was blond Jamie, the first boy at school to get a car; they had laughed, talked and fumbled now and then in the back of his Capri. He was married now with a wife, three kids, and a top of the range Shogun. Sheryl wondered if he still fumbled.

Martin never fumbled; he worked her body like a mechanic under the bonnet of a car, at least in the beginning he did.

'It's always good at the beginning,' Beatrice used to tell her. 'That's what people hold on to; and end up staying together for years just because it was good in the beginning. Why else would you scrabble about in the car with your ankles up by your ears if it wasn't good in the beginning?'

And of course, Beatrice was annoyingly right.

In the last year before the split, Sheryl figured she had spent most of her evenings waiting in front of the telly too scared to acknowledge that it was over. She threw herself into pleasing Martin, but by then his tastes had moved on, he had started to talk like someone from Kelvinside rather than Paisley, and Sheryl, with her pointy bra and leather bodices, had no effect on him.

She looked at him now with a couple of plasters over Sam's scratches on his face, and wondered, did he kiss Imogene like he used to kiss her?

'What do you think, Sheryl? Could you speak to Nefertiti?'

Martin ran his finger along her arm again, this time he lingered. She closed her eyes. 'Sail away with me, to another land, and we rely on each Other, uhuh…' crooned Dolly. Sheryl smiled, it felt so good.

Beatrice entered the bar fired with determination, and clattered into a set of chairs. Lindsey grabbed the back of her chair.

'What the hell's SHE doing with him?' hissed Beatrice.

'Ssssh,' said Lindsey, 'you got your darts?'

'I'll phone you,' said Martin, as Sheryl walked away. She said nothing all the time, wondering if he was staring at her arse.

Sheryl was walking away, because she had just heard the whirl of her mother's chair over good old Dolly Parton and Duncan's 'Way hay hay hay'. And as Beatrice crashed into her third chair, Sheryl decided the safest place to be was not with Martin, but with the belly dancers.

'What you doing, talking to that Martin the gorgeous?' said Beatrice.

Sheryl didn't answer; what could she say, Martin still fancied her?

69

She wasn't sure herself.

'Sheryl?'

'Martin was making me an offer I couldn't refuse.'

'Oh that!'

'He is under the ridiculous illusion that I can talk... you know? How do you know?'

'Lindsey told me; she has the same hairdresser as his new piece! Your sister fancies herself as an undercover something.'

'Damn it, Mum, why didn't you tell me?' Sheryl said.

'I thought if he surprised you, then perhaps you wouldn't be so amicable, maybe you'd be annoyed enough to actually stand up to him.'

'You wouldn't believe what he wanted me to do,' said Sheryl, smiling to herself.

'Nothing would surprise me about Martin. Did you stand up to him?'

'Yes!'

'What did you say? Did you tell him where to go?'

'Well, 'er no, not exactly!'

'Did you get some money off him?'

'No, not really, I just sort of walked off.'

Lindsey threw Beatrice a 'Don't forget what you're here for' look, and Beatrice decided for once to keep her mouth shut.

'Let's celebrate with a game of darts?' said Lindsey.

CHAPTER NINE

Conway sped his Fiesta through Glasgow, and by the time he was at Loch Lommond, he had worked up enough speeding fines to stop him driving for ten years. He stopped at Luss and opened his sandwiches. Bits of a cold fry up fell onto his lap, but Conway didn't notice, instead he stared out of the window, lost in dark thoughts, while a seagull circled above.

The seagull was persistent; it pecked and chased any other bird that came near. Conway looked down at his cold breakfast on his lap; he was so wired he couldn't even eat. He poured himself a coffee as the bird planted itself on his bonnet and stared in.

Conway revved up the engine and reversed. The unfazed bird hovered, and Conway, a little impressed with his persistence, emptied his breakfast on the tarmac. 'Just you wait, Archibald,' he muttered with a slight spray of coffee. 'I am going to make you and the rest of 'em eat their friggin words.'

****

Beatrice laid the darts on the table. Sheryl stared at their steely points glowing under the light.

'Perhaps I should go home,' she said, still staring. 'I've got an early start tomorrow.'

Beatrice placed a half pint and a double whisky beside her. 'Just one game won't hurt,' she said.

The bar went quiet. Duncan let out a knowing tut, then pushed his empty glass across the bar. Shifty refilled the glass with a shake of his head. He had plans involving an early finish, a couple of cans of

71

Export and Sky Sport. He watched Sheryl lift her whisky to her lips, and whistled through his teeth, not much chance of that now.

Beatrice pushed the darts closer to her, 'Just one for the road,' she said.

Mavis rolled her eyes to the ceiling, 'Sheryl, mind you got your wrestlers tomorrow.'

Sheryl said nothing; in one hand she had her darts and was meditatively rolling them between her fingers; in her other was her drink.

'Sheryl?' said Beatrice.

Sheryl looked from her mother to her darts, it had been so long. She sipped her whisky; one game wouldn't hurt, she took another sip and then with a look of inspiration, drained her glass.

Shifty sighed, turned the TV on to Sky Sport and poured himself a pint as Sheryl pushed her empty glass across the bar and walked to the dart board.

****

Sheryl woke up and stared at the cracked skylight as the odd snowflake danced about the outside. Just one game, she told herself, just one bloody game. She should have walked away, she should have known better, since when after a whisky has it ever been just one bloody game.

****

Sheryl remembered the wrestling was on TV, Steel Ice and Johnston were playing a tag team match against an Australian duo called The Crow and The Mad Budgie.

The Australian team entered the ring wearing florescent green and yellow Lycra, while swinging a didgeridoo to the tune of 'Tie me kangaroo down.'

Steel Ice came in on a Harley Davidson, with Johnston in a sidecar. Before the bell rang, they were in the ring breaking didgeridoos over their knees. The Crow and Mad Budgie didn't stand a chance.

Within minutes, Sheryl had beaten her mother with a double twenty, downed her second whisky and was ready for the next.

'Another game,' she said, Beatrice threw Lindsey an 'It's in the bag' look, and then ordered Shifty to turn up the TV.

Steven was standing by the scoreboard, watching Sheryl's darts slice into the board like a hot knife through butter, and he could hardly add up fast enough. Just as well, he thought as Uno Sumo, a large Japanese wrestler, had now appeared on the TV and the camera it seemed was fixated with his large rump barely covered by a g-string and tassels. It was enough to put a man off his diet coke.

Beatrice looked up at the TV and smiled, tomorrow was as good as hers.

'Now that is a bum a girl could get used to!' said Mavis. 'Large men make the best lovers; men who love food have a love for all things sensual.'

'I'm a big boy, Mavis,' said Duncan.

A chuckle ran through the bar, which stopped with a hush as Sheryl finished on a bull's eye. She pushed her empty glass across the bar to Shifty, who lifted and placed it under the optic, the ice had hardly melted.

'My ex had a large rump,' said Kay. 'And there was nothing sensual about him; watching him tuck into a plate of chips was enough to put any one off IT!'

'What about old Chinnie? He's well-rounded,' said Shifty. 'And your neighbour don't seem to mind. As soon as her man's out the door, he is in there like a ferret up a trouser leg.'

'Aye, but I've heard he's built like a horse,' said Kay.

'Tackle's not everything,' muttered Duncan.

Steven looked on, considering a hasty retreat. The mere mention of a man's tackle sent shivers down his back. Having grown up with three sisters, he had heard it all too many times. He got all his sex education through the walls of his bedroom, while staring at his action man comics. Thanks to his sisters, he knew what women wanted and what they didn't. To him, it seemed the prospect of pleasing a woman was as easy as the plumbing in Beatrice's house.

After three games, Sheryl ordered some sparkling wine and pork scratchings for 'all'. Everything was great in the world, and she just had to share it, Martin wanted her, she was playing like a dream (and beating her mother) and she was going to meet Johnston tomorrow. She was on a complete fucking roll.

Sheryl watched as her mother's chair circled about the room. She watched her mother's image split into two and wondered if the wine had been such a good idea, despite this, she smiled. Smiled at her mother and good ole Shifty and nice man Steven, perhaps she could give them a hug if she could just stop things moving in front of her. It was, after all, a nice world.

'One more game, Sheryl, winner takes all?' whispered Beatrice.

'Whaaat ?'

'Whoever wins chooses what to take.'

'A round like?'

'Whatever, dear.'

****

Sheryl stared at her wrestling poster on the ceiling in her bedroom; she should have known as soon as her mother uttered the words, 'Whatever, dear,' how things would turn out.

****

Sheryl staggered up to the board, what she didn't know was that Beatrice had been practising. Darts was one of the few sports left to Beatrice, and she had practised it with the same competitive spirit she attempted most things. Beatrice looked at the board, focused, and then threw a bull'seye. Sheryl was still on 150 when Beatrice hit her double, and Sheryl knew as soon as Beatrice won, what her 'whatever' prize was going to be.

'You okay?' said Steven.

'Huh?' Sheryl sat at the table staring down at a soggy beer mat. It was the only place to look that didn't make her feel dizzy.

'It's just that you have gone all white,' Steven continued, taking a seat opposite.

Sheryl mumbled as her mouth began to water. 'I think my mum just conned me.'

'You want a coffee?' he asked.

A certain familiar numbness began to spread down to her tongue and her teeth. She ignored this and as the sides of the beer mat began to sway, she ignored this as well and turned her glances towards Steven. She had never noticed how attractive he was before; he had the sort of slim figure that looked good in jeans.

'You're a LOVEEERLY MAN, Stevie!' she said, tapping her

75

fingers on his hand.

Beatrice looked across at her daughter. 'Don't take any notice of her, Steven, after half a bottle of whisky, she's anybody's!'

'Sheryl, you sure you don't want a coffee?' asked Steven, moving his hand away, what was it with alcohol and Sheryl?

'Yes. Er no...' mumbled Sheryl. 'I think I am going to be... sick!'

CHAPTER TEN

Martin woke up with a lot of questions and no answers. He looked towards his sleeping Imogene and sighed. Was Sheryl going to help or not? There was Rodger's show to open and all the right people were coming. He had the right wine and nice nibbles. What was he going to do if Rodger was still loopy? How could he show Rodger's work without Rodger? He needed him there to sign cards, chat up the clients and look interesting. He needed his consent.

This is an absolute nightmare, thought Martin; he cursed Nefertiti over his Espresso machine. 'What the hell is wrong with having your fanny painted?' he muttered. 'I mean, a woman her age, she should be grateful someone still wants to look at it.'

Martin looked in on Rodger lying on the couch, mumbling in French, he was a loony of the worse kind, unpredictable, impractical and totally smitten with a woman who thought she was God's answer to every man's fantasy. Did he mean what he said about burning every painting?

He had thought about cancelling the whole thing but there were more than fifty folk invited, and there were the pieces written by Imogene in the local papers, and The Herald for God's sake. He knew of at least ten folk who were coming from Glasgow. He shook his head and poured his second espresso, he needed caffeine bad, and he needed the coffee shakes to think.

Martin had met Rodger nearly three years ago. Martin had just brought Peek-a-Boo, which at the time was a run-down sewing shop with flaky grey walls and a boarded-up window. Martin had a vision for Peek-a-Boo; a vision that hopefully wouldn't cost too much, but captured the spirit of underwear with a difference.

One slack morning, Rodger had walked into the post office with 'his' Nefertiti on his arm and a giro in his pocket. He saw Martin bending over the counter looking at paint colour charts and shop fitting brochures, beside his elbow was a plan of the interior of a shop, and written in the corner was a title:

PEEK-A-BOO - UNDERWEAR WITH A DIFFERENCE

'My Rodger will do it for you,' said Nefertiti, leaning over the counter with a smile. Muriel sniffed, but Martin was definitely interested. 'My Rodger is an artist of great talent,' said Nefertiti 'and he's lookin for work.'

'How much does he charge?'

'Negotiable,' said Nefertiti, 'with the rent on my flat.'

Rodger transformed Peek-a-Boo into the sort of shop any woman could spend hours in. He fitted delicate lighting to make even the jetlag look fresh, and he painted murals of round bums and upright breasts that were the highlight of any man's walk down the main street of Lochgilphead. So when Donald, an elderly picture framer, came into the post office and talked about Rodger's latest works, Martin's ears pricked up. Donald was impressed by nothing.

'He's working on a collection of paintings called the Unveiling of the Flower of Scotland,' said Donald, 'and it's amazing.'

Martin had the rumblings of an idea, which he later had mulled over with Imogene.

'Since when has Donald called anything amazing?' he said.

Imogene was not impressed.

But Martin liked what Rodger had done with Peek-a-Boo, maybe his collection could work miracles with his new venture the, 'A Wee Bit of Art' shop in Oban? So Martin made Rodger a proposition and Rodger, under the influence of a few too many in the Argyll, accepted. Nefertiti was the last to know.

Rodger was sitting by the fire feeling sorry for himself. He looked at his bandaged hands. 'These hand will never paint again, as long as my bugle is unattended,' he muttered in French.

Martin slid a herbal tea across to Rodger. Rodger shooed him away with his hand and a few mumbled words.

'English, Rodger, remember?' said Martin.

'I am an artist,' yelled Rodger. 'I feel the pain of an artist.'

Martin sighed and sought advice from his now hopefully awake little "Haystack."

****

Conway arrived at Chubby's house, and within two grunts was sitting in the lounge room with his laptop open.

He clicked onto the Constable file. The Constable File was his albatross; the black cloud in his dull life, the chink in his armour that trailed behind him like a quiet fart in a small shop. He dragged the Constable file to every new station he worked in. Within a week, it was installed in his desk computer and then at any spare moment, it was up on screen. Conway never lasted long in one place.

'That will all change,' he mumbled to himself while ruffling through his box of notebooks. 'Just you wait, ole boy, I've got you this time.'

Chubby knocked on the door and entered with a tray of meat

sandwiches and black coffee, Conway didn't even look up.

'That's Nefertiti's man,' she said, looking at the screen.

'Who? What the hell kind of name is that?'

'A belly dancing name,' sighed Chubby.

'Hmm and where's he now, then?'

'Where she goes, he goes, he's like her little puppy.'

'He more than that,' muttered Conway.

Conway knew him as Eduardo Brassier. The biggest con artist this side of Glasgow. Eduardo made a modest living selling his paintings in a rundown antique shop, and he made a fortune selling fake masterpieces on the black market behind the said antique shop.

Eduardo painted artwork that he claimed were missing masterpieces, such as Vincent van Gogh's other chair, Matisse's poppy field in winter and Whistler's best friend. And he made a fortune because the people that bought them were too embarrassed to go public, until he met Conway.

Conway had walked into Eduardo's shop on a whim, it was a hot afternoon and his stomach was playing up. Eduardo offered him some peppermint tea.

Conway looked at the paintings displayed in the shop and for a while, his troubles melted and his stomach was soothed.

'I was an artist once,' he said.

'And what happened?'

'Mortgage, marriage.' Conway sighed and rubbed his stomach.

'Have more tea,' said Eduardo, the gods always brought him someone.

Two hours later, Eduardo took Conway around the back of his shop to a small shed.

'I found in old lady's house,' he said. 'It's what I do, someone dies, I clear out and sell what family don't want, I get a cut. This time, I ask for this,' he said with a Mediterranean gesture. 'It's Constable's, how you say? Back yard.'

Conway sucked in his breath.

Eduardo explained that he was moving back to France, he had BIG Bills, an angry ex-wife, 'And my children, they want to do the university.' He sighed. 'I make more money back home.'

Conway left with a huge hole in his bank balance, and an even bigger smile. Conway was proud of what he had bought, he was so chuffed he told everyone, including Edna.

'Constable's backyard?' she sneered. 'My arse, you've been conned.' Conway hung his treasure above his mantelpiece anyway; what would his wife know about art?

Conway was sure, so sure that he went on the Antique's Road Show.

'It's Constable's back garden,' he said to one of the experts, who with a gentle smirk tried to stop Conway explaining Constable's love of cabbages and beetroot to a large percentage of the television public. Conway never lived it down. It was the first time his wife sniggered while reading the paper, and the first time he, tight-lipped, brushed HER crumbs from the tablecloth and walked from the room.

Conway had gone back to the shop, but by then Eduardo had left, presumably to France. Conway started the Constable file and made it his mission to follow Eduardo and uncover his scam.

Chubby watched Conway eat the sandwiches within minutes, gulp down the coffee and produce a chorus of belches as if they were a work of great musical art.

'Rodger's at Martin's,' she said. 'I'll take you there if you like.'

Conway slid a couple of Rennies onto his tongue and headed for the car.

****

Martin watched his little Haystack get dressed, even with a bump she was still a sight to behold. He watched her apply her lipstick and truss her sweet round beasts into a red bra. He began to wonder when the morning sickness was going to vanish, his thoughts drifted to an afternoon in one of her father's farm shed, with just the smell of hay... *Think, must focus,* he thought, all this abstaining was beginning to have an effect on his concentration.

'My little Haystack, you know how Rodger and you connect on an artistic level?'

'The only thing I connect with at the moment is the bathroom.'

'This is important, we need Rodger on our side.'

She sighed; if only he had listened to her, they would not be in this pickle, if only he had gone with her choice; scenery is so in at the moment. But he had to go with genitals.

Imogene sighed as Martin gave her one of his, 'My sweet little Haystack' looks. 'I'll speak to him, then.'

****

Nefertiti didn't do cars, she didn't do old ladies either, especially ones like Beatrice. Nefertiti had decided to drive to Oban on her red, souped-up moped, well she did have a matching red leather outfit, and with all her stuff in Sheryl's car she could go faster.

Nefertiti was up early making coffee, by the time she had finished her second, Sheryl had emerged from the stairs looking crumpled, white, and very sorry for herself.

'You'll not be driving to Oban in that state,' said Beatrice.

Sheryl took a seat and put her head in her hands as Steven bounced into the kitchen with an annoying amount of energy.

'I have a nice packed lunch and...' He looked at Sheryl, 'She okay?'

Nefertiti slid on her matching gloves. 'Would you be a Darl and make sure she makes it, I need her. Nobody does lights like Sheryl.'

Nefertiti stood in the hall and gave herself the once over in the cracked mirror, ignoring the slightly distorted face, she figured she looked pretty good. She sighed for a moment and thought about Rodger, he usually did the music, he usually rubbed her back after a performance, she missed him. She stood to the side and held her stomach in, and then walked out to her moped.

Nefertiti flew down the main street of Lochgilphead and past The Stables, where sitting by the window was Edna and Mavis.

'That'll be herself then,' said Edna, stirring her milky coffee.

Mavis slipped a wee bit of whisky from her flask into both of their coffees. 'You ever fancy a go?'

'I had my fair share,' Edna laughed.

Mavis smiled the smile of a woman that had had more than her fair share. 'Didn't need belly dancing in my day,' she muttered.

Edna laughed again as they watched the red moped circle the roundabout and head off in the direction of the Oban road.

CHAPTER ELEVEN

'Damn it,' said Beatrice, 'they should sign post things properly, how was I to see that turn off?'

'Perhaps if you slow down a bit,' said Steven.

'That is the problem with this country, everything's just haphazard, millions of form fillers, and not enough workers, I mean, just look at the state of this road.'

She sped up and overtook a van; Steven took a sharp intake of breath as the car began to shake.

'You sure this car can take this speed?'

'Of course, speed clears out the engine. All cars need a good rev up.' Beatrice patted the dashboard, the car swerved a bit; Steven made a grab for the steering wheel. 'Sheryl fannies about in slow drive,' she continued, 'the pipes never get a good clear out.'

'Beatrice, this is a car designed for disabled people.'

'You got the better of the ex then, I think Sheryl was impressed,' said Beatrice.

'Oh!' said Steven, watching the middle white line of the road moving in and out. 'You know that you are supposed to drive to the side of that.' He pointed to the white line. 'Not over it!'

'He is the biggest fanny I've ever met,' Beatrice continued. 'What the hell she saw in him, I'll never know.'

'Yes,' said Steven, still staring at the white line, he figured if he watched it long enough, he could will the car to drive straight.

'Do you know he offered Sheryl another proposition?'

'A huh!'

'And did she turn him down with a mouthful of abuse? Not Sheryl, she just walked away.'

'How dignified,' mumbled Steven, closing his eyes. Maybe it was better if he didn't look?

'Oh,' said Beatrice, crashing the car over a deep pothole.

Sheryl pulled out her mobile and answered it. 'Hello? Oh is that you, George?'

Beatrice overtook a tractor, just missing an oncoming car.

'You know, we have ALL DAY to get there. Why not take your time? Enjoy the countryside?'

'Steven, it's raining.'

'What, I sound funny?' said Sheryl. 'No I'm okay, um...Beatrice is driving.'

Beatrice pressed harder on the accelerator, 'Is that George?' she asked.

'He wanted to know if we're okay.'

Beatrice grunted while staring at the road.

'He said to tell you to go easy on the car.'

'I know, I know he is always telling me that, damn it!' Beatrice wrestled with the steering wheel as the side of the car went up on to the verge then off again.

'He said to mind and keep between the two white lines!'

'Oh ha ha, very funny,' snapped Beatrice, gripping the steering wheel.

'I don't think he was joking, Beatrice, you're meant to drive on one side of the road, not the middle, maybe Sheryl could...' Steven turned around and looked at Sheryl's white face, and then looked back at the road.

Steven had heard a lot about Beatrice's driving, but never believed it could be so bad. He remembered George coming into the library white as sheet, muttering 'never again', as he shakily pulled out a hip flask and took a gulp.

Now Steven knew why!

He gripped harder on to the side handles by the door as they approached another bend.

'Ever thought of slowing down before you brake?' he asked in as casual a fashion as possible, as they screeched to a halt in front of a sheep.

'Why? I love speed. It's what driving is all about,' said Beatrice.

'But what about other cars, the other people? The speed limit is there for a reason!'

Beatrice snorted and then pressed the accelerator. Her reflexes were as good as the next man's, and her driving was a work of art, no one could push a car like her.

'Maybe you should call back later, George,' Sheryl mumbled, as she put her hand over her mouth and wound down the window.

****

George sat staring at his phone. Beatrice was driving again; he couldn't believe it. The last time Beatrice drove, he was following in the car behind. The Aces High Club had decided to celebrate Christmas in February with a visit to a pantomime in Glasgow, followed by a light supper afterwards. Beatrice had two members in her car (who never came back to the club), and George had another three, keeping up with her required the hide of an eighteen-year-old who thought he was immortal.

Yes, George decided something had to be done. Beatrice had no idea of fear until it was too late, then she crumbled, panicked and looked for a hero. He smiled to himself, he could be her hero; helping Beatrice out of bother was always so rewarding, watching her try to wriggle out of an apology was one of the best hobbies he had.

He decided to go to Oban.

****

'Stop the car!'

'What?'

'I said stop the car,' Sheryl mumbled through her fingers.

They were just by the turn off for Luing when Beatrice swerved the car to the side of the road, cutting off a cyclist, who staggered into a hedge. Steven, who happened to like cyclists, turned to Beatrice with a look she had never seen before.

'What the hell are you doing? What did that poor cyclist do to you?'

'He was too far over!' she snapped. 'Besides, when Sheryl makes a noise like that, time is of the essence.' She pulled into the side of the road with a smug sigh, 'Now that's what I call driving; fast or what?'

Sheryl staggered out, still making a noise through her fingers as she disappeared behind a tree.

'Fast, it's a wonder there's any rubber left on the wheels.' Steven stared at Beatrice. 'You ever heard of safety?'

'Driving fast sets my adrenaline pumping; I'm actually safer driving fast than slow. I'm much more alert.'

'I'm bloody well catching the bus from now on.' Steven jumped out of the car. 'I have never been so scared in all my life. What I sat through back there was not driving, it was nothing remotely like driving, that was abseiling across concrete. I saw my whole life flash before me.'

'Steven, I'm a good driver.' Her face reddened a little.

'Yes, if living is not that important!'

A police car drove by and slowed down as one of them took a note of Beatrice's number plate, no one noticed.

****

Conway stood at Martin's front door, impatiently knocking, 'Alright, Eduardo, I know you're in there.'

'What the hell?' mumbled Martin as he opened the door. 'Chubby? Who's this? What do you want?'

'I want to speak to Eduardo.'

'So.'

'He means Rodger,' said Chubby.

'Well, Rodger has important things to deal with in Oban, and he'll not have time for any of this crap.'

Conway flashed his police card in Martin's face. 'This aint crap, it's a police matter.'

'It says Paisley.'

Conway sighed. 'Look, just give me Eduardo, I mean that Rodger fellow, and then you can be on your way to sunny Oban.'

Martin glared at Conway. What the hell kinda jumped up git was he?

Conway stared back. He had met Martin's type before; he knew if he just kept staring, Martin would eventually give in. Funnily enough, Martin thought the same thing and as they hit gridlock, staring, Imogene came downstairs and began to look for Rodger. When the green corduroy jacket could not be found, she knew it was pointless. She pulled the front door from Martin's hands and stared from one man to the other.

'He's gone,' she said. 'And he has taken the car with him.'

****

Sheryl wretched herself dry, 'Oh God,' she moaned over a passing tractor. Beatrice remained in her seat and looked across at her daughter with the flat expression of someone who had never experienced a hangover in her life.

Steven stood at the road side, pretending not to hear, he looked out over the loch and wondered about survival and how he, along with everyone else, was going to make it to Oban in one piece.

****

Martin convinced Conway that taking him and Imogene with them to Oban was the best plan.

'That's where he'll be headin', to see his Nefertiti.'

'Or maybe he's gone to burn her fannies,' said Imogene.

Martin glared a 'Shut up' look at Imogene, for such a good-looking toff, she could be so coarse sometimes. 'And I know Oban like the back of my hand...' he said.

'There is not exactly a lot to know,' said Chubby.

Martin stifled a glare with a deep inhale.

'If we leave now,' said Conway, 'we will be able to catch up with the bastard.'

'He took the BMW,' said Imogene, 'that thing flies.'

'Depends who's driving it, HEN,' said Chubby.

'Don't call me hen.'

'I'll call you whatever the fuck I like.'

'If you call me whatever the fuck you like, then I'll not be coming, and as Martin says, I connect on an artistic level with that,' she looked at Conway, 'BASTARD. You need me.'

'Right, that's enough,' said Martin. He caught Conway's eye and within seconds, both men realised that despite an instant hatred for each other, to get what they wanted, they needed to work together.

****

'Get it up, girl,' yelled Beatrice, like a coach egging on a footballer. Sheryl threw her a menacing look then immediately regretted it.

'Here, Steven, give her this,' said Beatrice, handing over a flask. Steven gingerly handed it to Sheryl.

'If that is what I think it is, she can shove it,' said Sheryl.

Steven lifted the lid and sniffed it. 'Oh God, that's a ..'

'Raw egg in bloody brandy, my mum's latest.' Sheryl grabbed the flask from Steven and emptied it. 'That woman and her hangover cures. I'm sure it's one of her favourite pastimes.'

Nefertiti pulled up on her moped. She stood astride for a few minutes as if a photographer was about to appear, and then she walked over to Sheryl.

'How's my sidekick?' she said 'Any better? My God, how you gonna manage my lights, look at the state of yer.'

'Aye, well, alcohol is Sheryl's fools gold,' said Beatrice.

'What?'

'Drink gives her the illusion that everything is great, till the next day.'

Sheryl wiped her mouth and looked up. 'Perhaps if you didn't drive like there was a firecracker up your arse, I wouldn't be in such a mess.'

The phone rumbled in Sheryl's pocket. 'Where are you? We have lost Rodger.' Sheryl attempted to text Kilninver and gave up. She closed her eyes instead, and then immediately regretted it.

Beatrice tuned her radio to Argyll FM. Then, a little bored, she changed the channel to Radio Scotland. Maybe, she thought, she could ring George and tell him what a great driver she was? She looked at her watch; they were doing excellent time thanks to her. She could just see George's face once she told him how far they had come in such a short space of time, that would wipe the smile from his lips, and the 'Aces High Club', would they be impressed or what?

Sheryl rubbed her aching stomach, why the hell did she drink so much, she should have suspected something when her mother insisted on buying her whisky, the only time her mother threw whisky her way in such an abandoned fashion was when Beatrice was after something. She slumped onto the grass and closed her eyes.

'You ready yet, Sheryl?' yelled Beatrice. 'Come on, we are making good time!'

Flogging a dead horse sprung to Steven's mind.

Beatrice sighed and pushed a Neil Diamond CD into the player,

red red wine ...go to my head.

'MUM!'

Beatrice turned the volume up.

'ALL I CAN DO I'VE DONE BUT THE MEMORIES WON'T GO MY BLUE BLUE HEART, RED RED WINE...IT'S UP TO YOU ...'

Sheryl sighed and opened a can of Red Bull. She thought of all the hangovers she had had over the years, all the wasted days, all those evening when she had conversations with herself in front of the bathroom mirror, and now look at her, in front of nice man Steven, and bloody Neil Diamond. *Oh Bugger it,* she thought. *There has got to something better than this.*

Beatrice tooted the horn. 'Come on, girl, what are you waiting for?' she yelled.

Sheryl sipped her Red Bull and began to ponder on Johnston. 'Bugger it,' she said again.

'RED RED WINE ...DON'T LET ME BE ALONE.'

'Come on, Sheryl, Oban awaits us.'

'I don't think so!' said one of the two policemen as they walked across to Beatrice.

Beatrice let out a sigh and turned the music off just as Neil Diamond got to his blue blue heart again.

Their names were Gordon Rathbone and Roy Cocolder.

Rathbone was the taller of the two by at least half a foot, he had a kindly face and a small puff of bum fluff on his chin. However, it was Cocolder who did most of the talking; Roy Cocolder was a man with leadership qualities, a man capable of instant decisions and fair results, and a man who took control with a firm hand and no-nonsense approach; not easy with Cocolder for a surname, and a squeaky voice.

Beatrice, who was used to young men in squeaky voices, decided the only way to treat these men was with as much flippancy as possible.

'Is there a problem?' she said with a sweet smile.

Cocolder kicked one of the tyres.

Beatrice, using her polite 'Queen's English' voice, explained how many years she had been driving. She only began to argue when they looked under the bonnet like it was a peep show, oblivious to her comments, and then she yelled as they pushed and prodded the exhaust pipe. How could they question her abilities? AND accuse her of unsafe driving?

'Young man,' snapped Beatrice. 'I was not speeding.'

'You,' said Cocolder, 'were nothing short of a hundred.'

At last, someone with sense, thought Steven, who was still thinking about the cyclist.

'Nonsense,' snapped Beatrice.

Sheryl sat on the grass clutching her Red Bull can. Her headache had developed into a vice-like grip and her hands were beginning to shake..

Steven sat beside her, unusually quiet and grim. He had never been involved with the police before, and never had his insides been so tumbled by the fear of death as what Beatrice's driving had done to him. Steven looked across at Sheryl's profile; all this because she liked a dram or two-dozen after a crate of wine.

He moved a little from her side.

He had spent nights fantasising about making love under the stars while music from Swan Lake filtered softly in the background. He had pictured himself poised on top of her, looking into her eyes and whispering something romantic yet witty, as she looked into his. He studied her roman nose. For months, he had fantasised about tracing his finger on that nose, and other things along it. Just now, he thought it was the last thing he wanted to do.

Beatrice sat in stunned silence and wondered how anyone could question her driving. She was used to the comments her friends made, their pained looks and suggestions about Sheryl driving instead. But she always thought they were trying to be funny, or perhaps nice to Sheryl. Besides, what did they know about driving? But this policeman sitting in front of her was supposed to be intelligent; he was just downright rude, did he not recognise GOOD driving when it was right in front of his nose?

'Do you not know how fast you were going?' said Rathbone.

Beatrice looked at her nails. 'Well, I… think… speed is good for a car.' Her voice trailed away.

'Are you not aware of a speed limit then?' Cocolder's fingers drummed on the top of the car.

'Of course!' Beatrice said.

'And you,' he gestured towards Nefertiti.

Nefertiti smiled sweetly. 'I am an artist, a belly dancer.'

****

'So what's his work like then?' said Conway, driving through Lochgilphead.

'Nobody has seen it except Rodger and the framer; Mackintosh of MacTosser.'

'MacTosser?' asked Conway.

'Ahuh,' said Chubby, who went on to describe a man who hated paying for anything. 'MacTosser is the sort of guy who would short-change his mother,' said Chubby. 'He's tried it on with every shop in the area, and whenever he gets caught, he just tosses the rest of the cash over the counter.' Conway almost smiled. 'He used to be an artist,' she continued, 'painted nudes, mainly men, never sold many.'

'How?'

'They weren't very flattering. Let's just say men and cold studio sprung to most onlooker's minds.'

'But he said Rodger was amazing.'

'He's got a warped sense of humour,' said Chubby. 'God knows

94

what you will have to show.'

'I did warn you,' muttered Imogene.

'And he hates women.'

'I did say…' continued Imogene.

'Look, it'll be fine;' said Martin; all this talk of art was making him uncomfortable. 'Alls we got to do is find that Naff-arse woman and…'

'Nefertiti will never agree,' said Chubby.

'Everyone has a price,' said Martin.

'Not my Nefertiti.'

'Enough about that woman,' snapped Imogene. 'I'm tired of her and her fucking fanny.'

Conway and Martin sniggered, with the sort of snigger that sat comfortably in a pub, after a few, and purely between men.

****

'You see, my daughter has this drink problem, and I… and we are going to the wrestling and…'

'MUM.'

'You do realise you can't go about driving like some reject from a Dirty Harry movie!'

Beatrice sniffed; Clint Eastwood's was one of her least favourite actors.

'Give me your driving licence,' said Cocolder. He looked at it and passed it to Rathbone. 'You can't drive on this, it's way out of date.'

'What?'

'Out of the car, please.'

An uncomfortable silence fell on the group. Steven tried a little gentle persuasion 'Is that necessary?' he muttered.

'Step away from the car, sir, and let this woman out.'

'This'll be good,' muttered Nefertiti.

In silence, the police waited. Sheryl, still on the grass, didn't have the energy to explain.

Eventually, Beatrice snapped. 'I'll need my bloody chair then!' she said. Cocolder didn't even bat an eyelid.

Sheryl looked at the empty driver seat and sighed, she still felt ropy. She eased herself up and tried to look like she was full of life rather than dealing with a hangover. Rathbone, a man with a background in the Salvation Army, had served plenty of soup to such poor souls as Sheryl. He could smell a hangover a mile away.

He took Sheryl aside with a friendly warning. 'You get in that car and Cocolder will have you breathalysed.' He looked at Steven, Steven looked back, did he have a choice?

'You can't drive, can you?' said Beatrice.

'Well, I haven't for a while, but I have a licence,' he mumbled. Suddenly, Steven felt like a ten-year-old, trying to explain a good idea to an adult. 'Look, just because I ride a bike everywhere doesn't mean I can't drive, I have a licence.'

'But we've never seen you.'

'That's because I don't have a car. And, well, I prefer a bike, keep fit, like.' He coughed.

The women stared vacantly ahead as they mulled over the prospect of Steven driving, was it as good as his cooking or as bad as his DIY?

Steven, on the other hand, thought about Pugsy; the reason Steven never drove.

The day he got his licence, he had taken his father's car out of the drive and drove straight into the next-door neighbour's dog; Pugsy. Steven had heard a thump and a crunch followed by a howl as a black mass of fur was hurled up in front of him and smashed against the windscreen. Steven saw the black eyes stare back at him before they hit the glass and splattered, along with his jaw, (he was a heavy dog). He heard the scream from the little girl next door; he felt the thud of her fist on the side of the car, (she was large for her age) and then he saw the blood and innards ooze across the bonnet.

'You always hated my dog, you bastard!' yelled the ten-year-old.

The truth was he did, along with the ten-year-old, the fifteen-year-old brother, and the parents. Steven had been plagued by Pugsy for years. Every time Steven stepped out of the front door, Pugsy would bound freely from his lead and sink his teeth firmly into any part of Steven's anatomy. And there was never a witness, Pugsy was one hell of a smart dog, with a dislike for Steven, and an uncanny ability to stick his teeth into Steven's flesh without leaving a mark!

And it had only happened to Steven. The dog cooed at the postman, sniffed at his friends and rolled over for his sisters. Pugsy was nothing like his name, he was a massive black dog that looked like a cross between an English sheep dog and a pit bull. He had fur everywhere but around his eel-like eyes and jaw, and a bark that could be heard at the bottom of the street. Every morning, Steven woke to that bark. Thanks to that dog, Steven had a phobia for all things four-legged and noisy.

The day Steven drove out of his drive, he drove like a free man, like a man who would never have his butt bitten again. He drove fast; unaware that Pugsy was running across for a bite, that Pugsy didn't know he was in a car. The only thing Pugsy heard was Steven walking out of the front door.

Since that day, whenever Steven sat behind the wheel of a car, he froze as the apparition of a bloody dog loomed up on the screen, like something out of a Steven King movie.

'You can drive?' Sheryl said.

'Yeeees,' said Steven, trying to look confident.

'Well, that's great,' said Sheryl, trying to sound like she believed him.

Beatrice said nothing, she had seen him ride a bike and it wasn't a pleasant sight.

CHAPTER TWELVE

Steven drove off, not smoothly, but at least he didn't stall. As he turned on the ignition, an apparition of Pugsy appeared from the corner with innards dribbling from his mouth. *It's not real*, he told himself, when that didn't work, he tried some deep breathing. When that didn't work, he thought of Beatrice's driving, if he could sit through that, he could drive.

He turned the keys, switched the gear from park to reverse and just missed the front of the police car. He swore, pushed the gear into drive, held his breath and turned onto the road.

Beatrice pulled out her Neil Diamond CD and tuned the radio to Terry Wogan.

Nefertiti at first followed behind, but as that required sitting in second, she took to swerving in front and giving Steven the all clear at each bend than swerving back behind him; at least she was enjoying herself.

Steven was so nervous, his hands were covered in sweat and slipped on the wheel. He was hypnotised by the road and every little thing that passed by, such as a bird.

****

George stared out of his kitchen window, took a sip of his tea and smiled. *So they are staying in Oban*, he thought. He knew most folk in Oban as he had been born and bred there, and his sister Margaret stayed in the centre of the town. He figured he could stop at Margaret's for dinner, a few drams, a polite chat and then a walk to wherever they where.

Kerrie McLeod

The weekend was getting better all the time.

****

Sheryl is standing in the middle of the hotel ballroom dressed in a light blue and gold outfit. Her stomach is trim with no rolls. She looks around the room and there is no one there but Johnston, leaning in a leering fashion on a white piano. Behind him appears her Egyptian band. And they begin to play. She shimmies across the floor with a few hip flicks in between, and a very seductive backdrop. Before finding herself on the top of the piano doing a floor routine, somewhere along the line a snake is introduced, Johnston is mesmerised. The snake is as long as she is, and wraps itself around her hips and waist, she shimmies, then peels him off, lifting his head high above hers, and looking into his eyes as she does another back-bend. They then roll about for a bit before the snake slides down her body and off into the sunset.

Sheryl prepares for her finale. She begins with a back-bend on her knees and is just about to roll off the piano into Johnston's arms when the music stops, and the band disappears along with Johnston...

She falls painfully onto the floor and searches for him. Grabbing her silk skirt up into her arms, she runs barefooted through the hotel, down the long corridor, then outside just in time to see her hero step into the bus and shift along to the back seat between Nefertiti and Beatrice.

As the bus drives away, Sheryl runs madly behind, her costume tearing under her feet. She looks up to see Nefertiti and Beatrice waving and laughing out of the rear window, with Johnston leaning in a familiar fashion on their shoulders.

100

Sheryl woke up in the back seat of the car, with sweat pouring down her chest, and for a moment she thought it was all real.

The car swerved. 'Steven, it's a bloody leaf!' snapped Beatrice.

Sheryl looked around the car. They were just heading into Oban.

CHAPTER THIRTEEN

Steven drove the Volvo down the main street of Oban and pulled up just near the Caledonian Hotel. All the car spaces were blocked with red cones, except for one disabled space, which Beatrice spied through the crowd gathering in the street.

'Just in there,' she snapped, pointing to what Steven thought was a ridiculously small parking place. Steven tried and tried, and finally after a round of applause from the small crowd and a very sweaty brow, he parked just about a foot from the curb.

At the door, looking official in a navy blue porter's uniform stood a thin pale man. He watched what he would call an attractive-looking man finally park his Volvo. The porter walked over.

'Steven, you are a crap driver,' said Beatrice.

Steven said nothing. He had just spent the last half hour driving under the constant tutting of Beatrice, and for the first time, he understood Sheryl's need for a dram or twenty.

The porter knocked on the window.

'We are here, that's all that matters,' said Sheryl. She looked up at the old Victorian Hotel, it had really made an effort. They had American flags waving from the windows, and wrestling music blaring from somewhere, and a whole team of staff waiting outside the entrance, blocking any public going in. 'We actually made it!' she whispered to herself, and for the first time that morning, she smiled.

'And what is all this cock and bull stuff about dogs?' said Beatrice to Steven.

The porter tapped on Steven's window again. 'You can't park

here,' he said with an, 'I'm sorry but it's not my fault' smile.

'You are even worse at driving than you are at DIY,' said Beatrice. 'Is it absolutely necessary to screech to a halt every time we see a dog?'

'Look, the wrestlers will be here any minute,' said the porter.

Beatrice pointed to the disabled sticker. The porter looked at the grim-looking woman, whom he would describe as 'a poor man's Joan Collins', and decided that winning an argument with her was as possible as getting a suntan in Oban, so instead, he turned to Sheryl.

'I'm sorry, but we're fully booked, you can't park here.'

Sheryl smiled back, Beatrice unwound the window. 'We're to meet Harry,' she said.

'Harry?' muttered the porter.

And the wrestlers,' added Sheryl.

Nefertiti parked her moped neatly behind the Volvo. She stopped, posed for a moment then when no one apart from the porter seemed to notice, she walked over to the car.

'They're with me,' she said to the porter, 'they are my backstage hands.'

The porter smiled; he liked the look of Nefertiti. He had been in Oban a month now, and it wasn't often you met a woman who knew the virtue of good colour combination, especially a woman her age.

'Like your outfit,' he said.

'My name's Nefertiti.' She held out her hand. 'I'm the belly dancer. I'm to meet 'arry.'

Nefertiti explained about the wrestlers and her performance, she told him it was Harry who had organised it all. 'He promised a room for us,' she said, with a sweeping gesture of her hand towards Beatrice and company. The porter, who called himself Chas, elegantly whistled through his teeth. The truth was he knew Harry well. Harry was the sort of man who lived to the beat of his own drum. Time was like a foreign language to Harry.

'You could be here a while,' he said.

Steven got out of the car and huffed under the balcony of the hotel. Within two minutes, Chas had him down as one of those bookish types, with no TV and no girlfriend.

'Where did you get your licence from, an old folk's home?' yelled Beatrice.

'Unless you are nice to me,' yelled Steven, 'I am not driving you home.'

Her face reddened a little, 'If you're driving home, I'm not coming!' She pushed her door open, oblivious to any walking by, 'One of you gonna get my chair for me?' she snapped.

Sheryl walked around to the boot. She was feeling perkier by the minute, all she needed was a coffee and she would be almost brand new. She looked at the boot with a sigh verging on happiness. Each bag had been wedged in tight around a spare battery for the wheelchair, four breeze blocks, a small pile of slates and her toolbox. By the time she pulled her toolbox and a case out, she was almost singing.

Chas, being a nice fellow, took the wheelchair from Sheryl and helped the Joan Collins look-alike into her chair. Steven stood by waiting for his bad mood to subside. It didn't, it only smouldered very quietly, while the small crowd on the street developed into a large cluster of boys, mothers and elderly women.

Then a few of the crowd screamed.

'Oh my God,' yelled Chas. 'THEY'RE HERE!'

Steven looked up to see a bus appear with WRESTLERAMA plastered in florescent colours on the sides.

'Who?' yelled Sheryl, who was still pulling out the last of the luggage.

Steven watched as the bus pulled tightly along the front of the Caledonian. More people appeared from nowhere, some clutching autograph books and posters, others dressed in what Steven assumed was their favourite wrestler's costume. The door opened and the crowd screamed again.

'Look at that, Bea; it's them, isn't it?' said Nefertiti. 'Don't you just love them?'

Chas turned to Nefertiti, 'They are soooo MANLY AND BIG,' he sighed.

'I bet they aren't prissy about dogs!' Beatrice said.

'What's going on?' yelled Sheryl. She lifted her head as a group of boys ran by and knocked the car. The boot crashed down on Sheryl's head. Sheryl saw a few stars and then nothing, no one saw her faint.

Someone stepped out of the bus and the crowd, which by now had doubled in size, screamed louder. One of the commentators came out of the bus, followed by one of the Australian tag team wrestlers.

'G'day!' he shouted over the screams of the crowd.

'G'day!' shouted the crowd.

Johnston finally appeared in a gold and black leather outfit, which Steven noted looked like it had been painted on. And the crowd went wild, some (mainly women) threw knickers into the air. Johnston smiled, brushed a couple brightly coloured G-strings from his shoulders and waved.

'Is that Johnston?' said Beatrice to Chas. 'My God, he's gorgeous.'

'Definitely,' said Chas.

Nefertiti sighed.

Beatrice, using her chair as a plough, pushed herself to the front causing many to wince as she rode over their toes.

Steel Ice appeared from behind Johnston, and looked menacingly at the crowd then grabbed a pair of the knickers and rubbed it under his arm. The women booed as the younger members of the group pulled a face. He then rubbed it into Johnston's face. Johnston took a swipe at him, after which they fell to the ground with a lot of grunting.

'Get him,' yelled someone from the crowd.

'Put the boot in.'

'Yeah! Give it to him!'

'Smash his head in!' yelled an old lady from the back.

A few of the younger children cried.

'Oh my!' said Chas.

A few large men in suits appeared from somewhere and pulled them apart. More large men with WRESTLERAMA tee shirts and black tracksuit bottoms jumped from the bus and began to push the crowd back.

Steven looked on and wondered if it was not just a little extreme, staging a fight to avoid autograph signing.

Johnston and Steel Ice glared at each other. The knickers once flying in the air lay trampled on the ground. Steel Ice kicked a few about, treading them into the gutter and then stared at the crowd, causing some children to cry louder. A bouncer grabbed his arm; with a loud grunt he pulled away and took another swipe at Johnston, who crumpled to the ground. The rest of the other bouncers held back the women jostling for a punch at Steel Ice.

'Why don't you lot just piss off?' Steel Ice yelled, then stormed into the hotel.

Johnston, lying on the floor with more acting ability than a football player in the World Cup, grabbed a pair of knickers from the ground and dramatically wiped his brow and then with the aid of half a dozen minders, stumbled to his feet and waved to the crowd, before staggering to the hotel.

Sheryl came to with a thumping head and a grazed knee, she wondered where she was and how come her head thumped like it been hit with a hammer. Then she heard the screams from the crowd.

The crowd hustled to the entrance, looking hopeful but were stopped by the bouncers.

'Well I never,' said Chas, gripping the back of Beatrice's chair. 'I hope Johnston kicks his tight arse tomorrow.'

'Me too,' muttered Beatrice.

Sheryl stood up and wandered around the side of the car just as Johnston walked into the hotel, she saw the back of his head but was too dazed to recognise him.

'Did you see that?' said Nefertiti.

'What?' muttered Sheryl.

'We just saw Johnston,' yelled Beatrice.

'Rolling on the ground with Steel Ice,' said Nefertiti.

'And Johnston was wearing the most gorgeous leather outfit,' added Chas.

'It was so tight,' added Steven, 'that farting would have been impossible.'

Sheryl rubbed her head. 'You mean I missed Johnston?'

'You didn't miss much,' mumbled Steven.

'Look, there he is,' yelled someone from the crowd. He pointed to one of the windows.

Chas dropped his case and began waving frantically. 'He's waving.' Nefertiti struck a pose, while Beatrice started giggling like a schoolgirl. 'Yoo-hoo,' she yelled 'Over here.'

'He seems to have recovered from his beating,' murmured Steven.

'We love you, Johnston,' yelled someone from the crowd, as Johnston slid back inside.

Sheryl looked up at the window, causing her head to pound harder. 'Oh God,' she muttered and closed her eyes.

'We just saw Johnston …again!' said Nefertiti.

'And he waved,' laughed Beatrice 'To us!'

'That was just in our direction,' Steven grunted.

'He caught my eye.' Chas looked up again wistfully.

Sheryl stared in the direction of the bus then at the window. 'What happened?'

'He is sooo gorgeous,' muttered someone from behind.

'Oh I know, don't you just love a bit of rough?' said Chas.

Steven said little; there were many things he could think of to call a man who dressed like a prostitute, but rough wasn't one of them.

****

Jimmy the bus driver sat in McTavishes Cafe, with a plate of chips and a roll and sausage. He had seen many things in his time, but flying G-strings and men rolling on the pavement was not one of them, and certainly nothing he would write home about. He dribbled some sauce on his sausage. 'The whole thing's a cock up,' he said, with a wave of his roll.

'scuse me?' said the waitress, cleaning the table.

'The hotel, someone's over-booked; they offered Johnston and Steel Ice a family room with twin beds, and Uno Sumo a staff room, too good for 'em if you ask me.'

'You're with the wrestlers?'

The bus driver smiled and stabbed a chip into his brown sauce. What was it with women and wrestlers? The waitress put down her damp cloth and took a seat beside him as he talked about the intimate details of some of the wrestlers. 'They are moving some of 'em to another hotel,' he said. 'Maybe you can help with the directions?'

The waitress nodded her head and laughed, helping him would be her pleasure, she said. In fact, her shift would be over soon and she had nothing planned.

Jimmy walked back to the Caledonian with his wee tummy wobbling and his shoes clipping on the tarmac. He was thinking about the waitress and her phone number and how tonight might be a night to remember after all, when he noticed the Volvo parked behind his bus, and the crowd still milling around. Jimmy realised that moving the bus would be a whole lot easier with the Volvo out of the way, so he approached Steven.

Steven jumped into the car and turned on the engine. An engine that had been pushed to the limits by Beatrice, then stalled and started by Steven. An engine on it last legs and held together by a shoestring of second-hand parts. An engine that was over ten years old, and had bugger all life in it.

A small trickle of smoke escaped from the bonnet, followed by a hiss and the smell of burning oil.

'I'd get out of the car,' said Jimmy.

Steven, still thinking about the cyclist and other annoying things, didn't hear. He tried the engine again; it made a loud rumble and then a bang. Jimmy pulled Steven out of the car.

The milling crowd now formed a semi-circle around the car as a flame appeared from the side of the bonnet. Someone mumbled something about the fire brigade, as another appeared with a fire extinguisher and tried to get it to work. Steven stood back in his Boots position, and watched as a tyre hissed itself flat.

Timing, thought Steven, *it's all about timing.*

****

Conway's fiesta rumbled into Oban. As he braked at the lights, the back seat slid forward for what seemed the millionth time to Martin.

'You ever think of fixing this seat?' grumbled Martin.

'Oh that? It's been like that since I brought this car, hardly notice it now.'

'Ever think 'bout getting a new car.'

'You kidding? The wife hates this car; she won't even get in it.'

Before they hit the first roundabout, Martin ordered Conway to slow down and then pointed to the 'Wee bit of Art' Shop.

Conway pulled into a disabled car space and slapped a sticker on the windscreen.

Martin looked around; there was no sign of his BMW and no sign of life in the shop. The blinds were closed and the door was locked, but as they walked around to the back of the shop, the faint beat of Status Quo could be heard.

'The bastard must be in there,' said Conway. 'I'm going in.'

Martin followed, there was no way he was going to let this nutcase of a cop alone in his gallery, especially with the loony artist loose. There were thousands of pounds worth of merchandise in his shop, hopefully still in one piece.

They walked into the gallery to the sound of Status Quo pumping, a sea of unlit candles and flowers, and a small buffet of chocolates and wine; but no Rodger.

Predictable, thought Martin, *but for a Looney, quite disappointing.*

Conway looked around the gallery with the eye of a policeman; each of the paintings was covered with a sheet, and in the corner was a box that he took a guess to be a pyromaniac's toolbox. He opened the box; flammable liquid and matches. *Predictable,* thought Conway, *and for such an artist, very disappointing.*

Chubby tapped manically on the window.

The men looked up.

'Just saw Nefertiti,' she said, 'come on, he can't be far.'

Conway pulled another Rennie from his pocket, tossed it into his mouth and crunched it; within two bites it was gone and a small belch rumbled from what seemed his shoes.

'Nefertiti, sweetie,' he mumbled, 'you are my ticket to promotion.'

****

By the time the fire brigade had arrived, the front of the car was covered in flames, the tyres were melting and the small crowd had doubled.

'Never did like that car much,' said Beatrice.

Sheryl said nothing, *Why bother,* she thought, just as she was starting to feel happy... *Timing,* she thought, *is the arse of my life.*

A tow truck pulled up near the fire engine, it had

ARGYLL WEST RESCUE SERVICES

Scrawled across the side, with

You prang it we bin it!

Scribbled underneath.

It had been painted various shades of blue over various patches of rust, and as the mechanic jumped out of the cab slamming the door shut, various bits of blue painted rusty metal fell to the ground.

'Never did like that car much,' muttered Beatrice again.

Steven shook his head. 'I thought Volvos were supposed be the safest car in the world.'

'A car can only take so much,' said the mechanic. 'To burn out the electrics,' the mechanic whistled through his teeth for effect, 'takes some doing!' He pointed at the bottom of the form for Sheryl to sign and then flipped over the page. 'You the driver?'

Steven and Nefertiti looked at Beatrice.

Sheryl pulled the mobile from her bag and read through the selection of text from Martin. It seemed Rodger was still missing, with Martin's BMW, and they were now in some burnt-out Fiesta with some 'bastard' called Conway. She sighed and then phoned George.

Timing, she thought, and then she couldn't be arsed thinking any more.

****

Conway and Martin at the same time came up with the same idea, Chubby would be the best person to stay and watch /guard the merchandise. She was big, strong and an expert with any sort of hitting/sawing implement.

'You're the perfect person to guard the gallery,' said Conway putting the pyromaniac toolbox in his boot.

'And we need Imogene to connect with Rodger,' added Martin.

Imogene sighed, another ride on the moveable back seat, what a way to spend a Saturday.

Chubby stood huffing on the pavement. *'And what would a calligrapher know about connecting?'* she thought, *except maybe joined up writing.* She wanted to look for her Nefertiti, she wanted to see the wrestlers. She watched the fiesta drive off with a jolt, and Imogene's long face wince as the back seat lurched forward, and then she walked inside the shop.

Chubby poured herself a glass of wine, slid a chocolate into her mouth and put her feet up. By the time she was on her second glass and fifth chocolate, she was feeling relaxed. She looked around the gallery, nobody would mind if she had a peek, would they? How would they know?

****

The word had got out that some of the wrestlers were moving to another hotel. The crowd outside was getting bigger, and many managed to sneak past the bouncer and get into the foyer. Thanks to Chas, Beatrice and Co. were already in the foyer tying to attract the attention of the receptionist. Finally, in desperation and habit, Beatrice sped her chair across the foyer, oblivious to the toes around her, and crashed into the reception desk. The desk shook a little and a few papers were ruffled, but still the receptionist didn't notice. She had too much to do.

Every now and then, the lift door would open and there would be a rustle in the air, a rush of fans and a knicker or two thrown in the air followed by a scream ending in disappointment, as some poor unsuspecting person would step out of the lift.

Chas was doing his best (in a useless fashion) to police the situation. His job was to keep control of the knicker situation. He spent his time confiscating the odd bag of underwear from some shamefaced woman, and pointing to the sign above the receptionist desk.

THROWING OF UNDERWEAR IN THE HOTEL FOYER IS STRICTLY FORBIDDEN.

But nothing seemed to keep control for long; even the bouncers had trouble.

'Look, here they come again,' said someone from behind, pushing past Sheryl.

The crowd that was shuffling in front of the lift parted in the middle as the doors of the lift opened and two heavy-looking men stood in front of a six-foot blonde. The crowd from behind jostled past Beatrice, pushing her against the wall; she had no time to manoeuvre,

'There he is!'

'WHO?' shouted someone else.

'Johnston, I think.'

'Who?'

'It's Steel Ice!' shouted a voice from the back.

There was a scream and a couple of women fainted. Sheryl caught a glimpse of a blonde head.

'I think I saw a wrestler, Mum,' she said, her stomach ws doing somersaults.

Beatrice stretched to look, but could only see a wall of backs. She watched her daughter crane her neck with the look of childish excitement. 'I can't believe it, I saw the head of a wrestler,' said Sheryl. Beatrice sulked in her chair.

The blonde stood for a few minutes waiting for the men in front to move. She wore a tight skirt, so short that any movement apart from careful walking would have been indecent. Her blonde hair was pulled back into a plait swinging down to her waist, and in her hand she held a black whip, which she tapped against her thigh now and then. Steven looked at her knee-high boots, strapped and buckled. He looked at the pulled-in waist tucked into a three-inch wide belt, and the observably big, gravity-defying bosom, tipping over the top of her bodice, and he whistled through his teeth.

She cracked the whip on the ground, and the crowd parted, then she walked forward, tapping the side of her leg again with the handle of the whip.

What the hell kind of sport is this? thought Steven.

The crowd was stunned into silence as she walked, then out of the shadows of the lift came Johnston, dressed in black and pink leather, with five heavies beside him.

Sheryl watched Johnston walk by; she caught a glimpse of his shoulders; his profile and his smooth hair hanging down his shoulder. She saw his chest exposed beneath the open pink shirt, glistening under the florescent lights of the foyer, and she sighed. He walked like a man of action, like a king through his people.

The crowd followed as he walked to the bus, and they chanted his name as it drove away.

Beatrice missed it all; the only thing she saw was the back of a few fans and a wee glimpse of some blonde piece, and as the crowd dispersed, she stared ahead.

'Pink?' said Steven, 'What kind of man wears pink?'

****

Beatrice did notice another man walk towards them. He gave her a wave and a full set of new dentures smile. She watched his round stomach peep through a tight lemon suit, and wondered how many years of good living it took to produce such a body.

'You must be Nefertiti,' he said to Sheryl, while looking at her chest.

'I AM,' said Nefertiti, annoyed that he wasn't looking at her chest.

'I'm Harry,' he said, stretching out his hand for a handshake. 'You've been sorted yet?'

The four of them looked at Harry as if he was the village idiot. 'You think we'd be here like this if we were?' said Beatrice, nodding towards their luggage.

Harry slid his hand into his pocket, and with a sympathetic smile, explained about 'the mix up'. 'I've got a nice B&B for you; good friends,' he said, using the words 'homely' and 'welcoming'. What he didn't say was that the nice B&B had been his last hope.

Harry had arrived an hour earlier, while Sheryl and Co. were watching the Argyll West Rescue Services winch the Volvo's carcass onto the truck, he had slipped into the staff entrance of the hotel and was grabbed by Chas, among others.

'I've got a belly dancer, a pensioner in a wheelchair, and a gorgeous guy waiting to move in, seems you promised them a room.'

Shit!' said Harry as he pulled out his mobile phone.

116

Even before Harry dialled his first number, he knew it was pointless, there was a music festival on in Mull that weekend as well as the wrestling, and everywhere was booked up. In the end, as a last resort, he had turned to Derek and Rona, friends of Chas.

'Give 'em a good offer,' said Chas, 'and they won't refuse.'

'My limo is outside,' smiled Harry.

'Limo!' said Steven, as his face lit up at the thought of a proper driver and car. He wondered about miracles and, if by some small chance, Steel Ice would beat the living crap out of Johnston.

****

No one noticed the BMW a few yards down the road, or the strange man in a green corduroy jacket inside. Rodger had just watched his Nefertiti get into a limo with that strange woman, Beatrice. He had the rumblings of a plan, which involved a bit of sneaking around, a bit of charm and hopefully, his bugle's wee hat. A plan this time that would not fail, all he needed to do was iron out a few details.

****

Chubby had polished off a bottle of wine and was now thinking about opening the second. She was laying spread out on a set of cushions in the middle of the gallery, with Status Quo on repeat, while she studied each painting; she was in heaven. Rodger's paintings reminded her of her first time, her first love, a feeling she hadn't felt in years.

She was looking at the work of a man who had spent a lot of time studying his subject. She was looking at a vision of beauty, a vision of lust, a vision painted by a man who had spent ages 'down there' and was quite happy to spend even more time 'down there'. A man who worshipped and tasted the best place God had created, and now wanted the world to see, in colour and enlarged, what he lived for.

'To the flower of Scotland,' said Chubby, while raising her glass and pulling out her mobile.

CHAPTER FOURTEEN

It was 5.00 o'clock when George arrived at his sister's house. He walked in from the cold to a dram, a plate of curry and his sister, Morag sitting by the fire with a grim 'What ARE you up to' look on her face.

'That was quick,' she said. 'What's the hurry? Beatrice?'

He said nothing but slipped his shoes off, poked the fire and took a sip of his dram.

'What car is it this time?'

'Volvo.'

'Are they not indestructible?'

'Nothing is indestructible in her hands!'

'I take it she'll not know you're coming then?'

'No, but this time I am going to win!' he said.

'If Beatrice was going to marry you, she'd have done so by now,' said Morag, placing a bottle of whisky by George's side.

'Marry? Who's talking about marrying? We are going to live in sin,' he said, and poured himself another Royal Brackla. 'The Marilyn Monroe of malts,' he whispered, and smiled. Life was all about timing.

CHAPTER FIFTEEN

Rona had bought the Boarding House Lochfeta when she had retired from the Council; it kept her busy and funded her and her partner's passion for visiting Clara's pub (a local pub on the pier). Usually, it was workmen who stayed all week and left at the weekend. But thanks to Harry's persuasive offer, Rona agreed to put up Nefertiti and her group for just one night during the weekend.

'I suppose we'll need matching sheets and coffee sachets,' said Derek, Rona's partner.

'With the money he's paying, they can have filtered,' said Rona.

Derek went to the cash and carry and bought stuff that he thought might posh up the place a bit. 'I'm not stopping, mind,' he said. 'Tonight's karaoke at Clara's pub, and a bottle of Whyte & MacKay is one of the prizes.'

Rona changed the beds and hunted out for matching cups. She had just finished spraying the air freshener around when Harry knocked on the door. A toilet flushed in the background as she opened it, and it continued to flush right through their conversation.

'Does that thing ever stop?' said Beatrice.

Rona sighed and shook her head. That cistern had been the bane of her life. It hadn't stopped flushing since they had moved in. Derek was of the age where prostate problems were, looming and the constant filling and flushing of the cistern did nothing for his 'problem'. Every morning, Rona would wake to the feel of her lover by her side and a smile on her face. As he woke, he would wrap his arms around her waist, and pull her into the curve of his body, just as

120

his lips would find her neck, the toilet would start flushing and Derek, with a groan, would jump out of bed.

'Many have tried,' Derek mumbled, before trotting off to the loo.

Rona watched her man disappear down the passage.

'Let Sheryl have a go,' said Nefertiti. 'She's amazing. Just look at those arms.'

Rona looked at Sheryl's robust body with little expectation. Of all the workmen who had trailed in and out, none had had any success. Many had tinkered and groaned over the old cistern, and yet none could solve the mystery. So the rhythmic flushing and filling remained, intruding into the atmosphere like music in a supermarket.

Rona looked at Sheryl's pasty face, and knew an earnest soul when she saw one, 'Would you like a cuppa and I'll show you the problem,' she said.

****

Sheryl downed her third cup of tea and looked at Steven, who was grimly staring ahead.

'You want another?'

'No!'

'You gonna help me?'

Steven shrugged his shoulder and said nothing.

He was tired and his insides were giving him hell, his mood had not really improved even with the ride in the limo. He thought about the next few hours. Whichever way you looked at it, it was not going to be fun. He looked outside the window and wondered how the cyclist was.

Sheryl crouched by the toilet, it was an old toilet similar to the one at the bottom of the stairs in Beatrice's house, and just like Beatrice's, it was surrounded by white tiles stained with age. Sheryl pulled a wrench from her tool bag and felt a little more in control. Rona stood by, watching as Steven silently handed Sheryl some sort of connection. Rona tried to fill the silence with talk, most of it about Harry and his balls-up.

'Oh well, our car blew up, how much more of a balls-up can you get than that?' said Steven.

Sheryl muttered something about her mother's driving and stuck her hand into the cistern.

Steven snapped. 'If you could just contain yourself to one bottle of wine instead of a crate, your mother wouldn't have had to drive, or me for that matter.'

'What?'

'Most people see a pre-dinner drink as a glass or two, not a bottle or more.'

'I knew an alcoholic once,' interrupted Rona, 'he was good at plumbing too'.

'Why do you need to get so drunk?' Steven continued, 'You are much nicer without it?'

'He's dead now,' said Rona, 'trying to hide some evidence.'

Sheryl pulled up the ball cock; it had been a long time since anyone had called her nice.

'He was unloading a supply of stolen bathroom furniture when he slipped and choked on an imperial mint. He was found on his back; arms still wrapped around a fine Victorian toilet,' Rona yelled from the kitchen. 'Apparently, there was enough whisky in his system to lubricate a funeral. Poor Mc Vain; he was a Scot, you know?'

Sheryl turned off the water and looked underneath the cistern, she ran her finger over some leaky joints and adjusted them.

Steven could not remember a time when Sheryl was not either hung over, or sculling alcohol. He could not understand her. Here was a woman built like an Amazonian Goddess, who made Charlie Dimmock look like a wimp. A woman who was equally at home with a fuse box, as a set of pipes, and scaled roofs like a trapeze artist? Yet this same woman could not stop after one bottle. Let alone one drink.

'You ever thought of joining the AA?' he said, trying to sound casual.

'Mc Vain joined the AA, didn't do him any good!'

Sheryl attempted a laugh.

Steven said nothing, what was it with drink and Sheryl? He had only ever been drunk once in his life. He was fourteen years old and downed a whole bottle of red Martini just because he liked the taste of it.

It was at one of his parents' parties, which he had cooked for. He remembered sitting at the kitchen table admiring his handiwork. He poured himself a glass and tasted it, it was like a smooth Ribena and it went down easily. Before he knew it, half a bottle was gone along with a plate of sausage rolls and half of the smoked salmon quiche, and his parents, who were by this stage dancing in the lounge room, hadn't even noticed. Steven found himself being sociable and even enjoying himself. By the time a third of the bottle was left, the salmon quiche was beginning to repeat a little.

'I'll just finish this off while I tidy up a bit,' he mumbled out aloud, (he was a tidy teenager) and that was the last he remembered …

Well, the rest he tried to forget.

While trying to clean in what now appeared two sinks, Steven downed the rest off the bottle, and then staggered into the party declaring his undying love for one of his mother's friends, who owned the newsagents down the road. As she stood by the fire singing, Steven took her hand in an exaggerated manner and then threw up all over the glass table. The music stopped as small pieces of red-coloured sausage and salmon dripped on to the white carpet beneath.

Steven spent the rest of the night bundled up in his bed hugging a bucket, while struggling to keep his eyes opened so as to avoid his head spinning.

Yes, he had been there, and once was enough. The painful months that followed with the nod and winks from his sisters, the jokes from his father, and the embarrassing blushes every time he met his mother's friend were just too much.

It took him three months to walk into the newsagents again.

Steven watched Sheryl's red hair fall about her shoulders as she crouched by the bottom of the toilet, with all the ease of a Middle Eastern peasant.

Steven sighed as familiar feelings of passion stirred in his loins. How he loved to watch her work, and act rough with a joint or two. How he loved to watch her strong arms work miracles with tools and grease. *A lady plumber who solved murders*, he thought, *that'd be a good next book.* She could come across dead bodies and clues while attending to someone's boiler. He smiled, he felt a bit better, he could just see his character; a wise-cracking tough red-head. He pulled out his note book.

With a tool bag slung on her shoulder, Sheryl marched into the castle.

Many stories had been bandied about the village about the old mansion, but none scared her. Sheryl had a job to do and bills to pay.

Her heart had been broken and the only way she knew how to deal with it was to work, and no ghost was going to stop her doing her job.

'You want a cup of tea?' Rona asked, already jiggling a tea bag up and down.

Sheryl slid a strand of hair behind her ear and stood up.

Steven watched Sheryl's shapely thighs straighten, then added more to his notebook.

Porter watched her from the window; he knew what she needed, a man of tenderness, a man who listened and understood, a man comfortable with the needs of a woman, and he was quite willing to find out what those needs were.

In silence, they listened to the cistern filling. 'I think it's sorted,' said Sheryl, with a gulp of her tea. Rona offered her a biscuit. Steven watched her dunk a garibaldi as the water in the cistern reached the top, they held their breath and silence followed.

'Another biscuit,' said Rona, with a wave of her biscuit tin.

Sheryl took another.

****

Derek was so chuffed that the toilet was fixed, he decided to take them out for a meal at the Fish is the Dish Café. 'They do the best fish and chips in Argyll,' he said, 'and you get a plate full.'

Steven had pictured candles, music... strawberries, and some lamb fillet slices sitting in one of those sweet sauces written about in a cookery book. He had pictured a small restaurant with stone walls, a wooden floor, and a very pleasant waiter... real coffee, handmade Turkish delights, and Sheryl dressed in some silky 'Eastern number' with perhaps just enough wine to perform a belly dance.

Instead, they were going to a chippy, which would probably be playing Scottish tartan music in the background, and serving stewed tea in glass mugs with UHT milk and dairy whip over frozen desserts.

Steven was beginning to lose hope.

****

Conway and Martin walked into the empty foyer of the Caledonian Hotel. There was a quiet hush present, the sort of hush created after a whirlwind of commotion has been and gone, leaving paper and rubbish crumpled on the floor. Conway stepped over a couple of knickers and walked up to the reception.

'You got a belly dancer staying here?' he said.

The receptionist fixed him a mean stare as the "no underwear" poster that had been grimly hanging on to the wall tumbled on to the floor.

'No, just a few wrestlers who want iced water with everything and think a cup of coffee is bottomless.' She sighed, she was supposed to have finished two hours ago, but thanks to Harry, she was still working and the room service list was getting bigger.

Conway, a man with minimum people skills, never noticed that she was tired and fed up; he only knew what he wanted. He pushed his police card across the desk.

'Just answer a few questions,' he said.

Martin attempted a smile and some (he thought) charming banter, which had little effect on the receptionist. She had seen enough banter in her time to recognise piss, when she saw it and as far as she was concerned, Martin's banter was piss weak. It was banter from an older man who had lost the ability to pull years ago. Banter that she listened to every Friday night behind the bar. Finally, she called the manager.

'There's no Eduardo or Rodger here,' said the manager, handing back Conway's card.

The manager talked about being snowed under with work, thanks to Harry and those damn wrestlers. He talked about Cocolder the local policeman, who was his son-in-law, and his daughter, who had a law degree. When Conway still looked like he was planted there for the night, the manager threatened to call Cocolder and his daughter, who by now had an honours degree in law.

Martin dragged Conway out of the hotel wondering about Conway's sanity. 'Call up that sister of yours, maybe she'll know where they are,' he said. 'She seems to know everything.'

Conway stood on the pavement listening to the messages from Chubby. There were more than ten, and with each one Chubby was drunker, for a moment, he, wondered about his sister's sanity, then he gave her a call.

'Fannies "R" Us,' she giggled.

'It's me, what the hell you playing at?'

'It's amaaaazing in here and I never realised how good a painting could be and how HOT Status Quo were. Why, they aaaaaare the DOG'S BOLLOCKS, just listen to this...

down down dedum down get down dedum down I wanna know.'

Conway looked confused. 'That woman should stick to meat,' he muttered. Martin grabbed the phone. 'LOOK, YOU GOT ANY IDEA WHERE THEY'LL BE ...THEY AREN'T AT THE HOTEL?'

'WHAT...HANG ON ...' said Chubby. She disappeared for a minute as the music was turned down. 'Helloooo you still there?'

'Yes.'

There was a long pause.

'Well?' said Martin.

'What?'

'You any idea WHERE they might be?'

'Oh that....' said Chubby. She looked at her watch and waited for her eyes to focus. 'Let me see,' she said with a stagger. 'It's sevenish, isn't it?'

'Yeeees.'

'Weeeell... I recon... they'll be... heading for the wrestling.'

'Which is at....'

'The Corran halls; shall I come?'

The two men yelled 'NO!' in unison, and then looked at each other, a little surprised.

Martin hung up then thought for a minute. 'You better get round to the shop,' he said to Imogene. 'She's as pissed as a fart.'

Imogene glared from one to the other, 'I am pregnant, you know, I should be putting my feet up.'

'Unless we get this sorted, there'll be nothing to put your feet up on,' snapped Martin. 'Now get down then and sort that dike out.'

Imogene said nothing but quietly walked down the road. She had never been spoken to like that before, and now she had to feed coffee to an overweight butcher who fancied anything in a skirt, except her.

****

The manager called Cocolder, who wasn't surprised. Cocolder, while answering the phone, was also standing by the fax machine reading an urgent fax from Archibald McConical. What Archibald McConical had to say didn't surprise him either. In fact, nothing surprised Cocolder. He was that sort of man unmoved by circumstances, when a crisis came along, he just moved his little body faster.

****

Steven looked across at Sheryl trying to make the best of things. They were sitting in the Fish is the Dish café. It was full of locals with a queue outside the door. The table were decorated in easy to wipe blue and orange plastic cover, and so close together that the waitress had to be a size eight to do her job. Steven watched as the waitress came through with two plates of huge battered fish and crispy chips, his stomach was feeling better, almost hungry.

On the other side of the room sat two young women drinking vodka and cokes, one with blue-black dyed hair who was called Helen, and the other was Joanna. They sang in Clara's pub at the weekend after a few too many, in fact, that's where they were heading after their supper.

'How's you?' said Rona.

'Just fine,' yelled Joanna, she slid one leg across the other and a small hint of a tattoo peeked from the hem. For once, Steven was glad Sheryl usually wore trousers.

Derek, still chuffed about the toilet, told the two women about Sheryl's miracle DIY. They were impressed; they had spent a few sessions in the Boarding House and the toilet did nothing for a bladder full of more than a couple of pints. The owner, Charlie McPherson, was also interested; he put his last bucket of chips into the fryer, ordered the young boy to watch and came over to the table, wiping his hands on his apron. 'I've a sink that needs seeing to and I can't get anyone,' he said.

'This woman fixes the unfixable,' said Derek.

'You any good at heating?' said an elderly woman with a tight perm.

129

'Sheryl works miracles,' said Steven.

'Just look at those arms,' said Nefertiti, 'robust or what?'

Sheryl wrote down her number and passed it around. She liked the idea of fixing things for folk.

Charlie talked about telling his customers or 'spreading the word', if she was any good, he talked about the need for good tradesmen in the area. The elderly lady with the tight perm and her two pals nodded, Sheryl looked like the sort of person they would like in their kitchen. 'You'd feel safe with someone like her,' muttered one of them. The others nodded. Sheryl looked like the type of person who would leave a tidy job and not swear over a smoke in the process.

Beatrice tutted while wheeling her chair in and out a bit to fit the table, 'You've not finished my house yet,' she grumbled.

'But this is paid work.'

'I put a roof over your head and this is the thanks I get.'

'You could get a van,' said Nefertiti.

'Paint the sides with your name,' said Steven.

'There are plenty of firms already,' said Beatrice, 'and you're no good with figures.'

Sheryl looked at her mother. Whatever parade she went to, Beatrice would always find the rain.

'I'm good with figures,' said Steven. 'I could help you with the pricing.'

Sheryl looked at Steven, spreading 'real' butter on to his bread, and for the first time she actually believed him. 'That's great,' she said and poured out the tea.

****

The Corran Halls car park was empty except for the

WRESTLERAMA bus, which was parked at the side entrance. Rodger drove in and opened up his Chinese take away, he needed a full tummy to ponder.

He spied American-looking people walking into the side entrance. After finishing his sweet and sour, he rolled his bugle's hat into a knapsack and walked into the side entrance. He wasn't quite sure what he was going to do, but he knew it involved his bugle's hat.

It wasn't long before he met a tall lanky 15-year-old called Bert, sitting disgruntled outside a changing room with a panda suit by his side and a script.

'I am a drama student,' said Bert, 'and look what they friggen want me to do.'

Rodger saw a light, a vision. He saw the finer details of a plan emerging, he pulled up a chair by the drama student and put on his listening face.

****

'I am just stating the obvious,' grumbled Beatrice. 'I mean, you managed Peek-a-Boo and it wasn't a great success, was it?'

'That was Martin's business.'

'Aye, well, you were stupid putting up with him,' said Beatrice. She turned to the elderly woman with the tight perm and turned up the volume. 'Married, you know. My daughter was seeing a married man.'

'I told you it was an open marriage and I'm not with him any more.'

'But you'd go back tomorrow if he clicked his fingers.'

Sheryl stared at the bowl of individual jam portions; and wondered again just how loud her mother's voice could get.

'It aint easy walking away,' said Nefertiti, 'it took me twenty years.'

'I thought you said he died.'

'I was lying,' said Nefertiti, gazing at the menu. 'Never trust a bloke that turns 'eads.'

'What?'

'Someone that everyone likes, you never see 'em. Do you know, I was the last person he wanted a coffee with; he would rather go to the dentist than sit opposite me in a café. Alls he wanted was his dinner at five and clean undies. Then he was off out with a fag in one hand, and not even a grunt goodbye.'

A trim schoolgirl with slicked back hair and a waitress apron appeared.

'His idea of foreplay was half a bottle of whisky and a Chinese take away, followed by a 'you wantin your hole?''

'Haddock or cod?' muttered the schoolgirl.

'Dunno why I put up with it.'

'Scampi,' said Beatrice.

'He got the 'ouse, the cat, the Christmas cards, and the sympathy. And I spent the next two years with no phone messages 'cept for those selling you cheap mobile phones.'

'Battered or breaded?'

'Nobody likes somebody who does what they dream of, especially women. All my friends ended up consoling me husband.'

Sheryl answered the phone, it was Martin.

'That bastard with you?' he said.

Beatrice looked at her daughter and clicked her fingers.

Sheryl hung up. 'I stayed with Martin cause I hated being on my own.'

'I'll have the haddock,' said Steven.

'Me too,' said Nefertiti. 'Suddenly, you're in the Co-op with a basket instead of a trolley, realising there is no one to go for a walk with.'

'Every weekend is the same,' muttered Sheryl.

'I know, teddies by your bed, museums for one, and a crappy film on a Saturday night.'

'And pissed men who fall asleep just after they've asked you for a shag, and you haven't even had the chance to tell them where to stuff it.'

'My Rodger didn't need a drink,' Nefertiti sighed, 'he just needed his bugle's hat and some music.'

The schoolgirl waited, 'What do you want?' she said to Sheryl.

'Fillet steak and Johnston,' said Sheryl.

'Don't be absurd,' said Beatrice.

'Cod then,' she finally said.

The waitress stood for a bit writing then paused. 'Um sorry, I forgot, the cod's finished.'

'I guess it'll be the haddock then,' said Sheryl.

****

While Sheryl and company were tucking into battered fish, Harry was finalising the promise of tickets for Beatrice and Co. Thanks to Beatrice's wheelchair, they were in the front row just by the commentators. Harry couldn't wait to tell them, especially Beatrice. Harry liked helping people. Harry was what was known in the trade as a 'people person', unfortunately, at times he liked them too much, so much so that he had a string of ex-wives and children, and not much control over his finances.

Harry arrived at the Fish is the Dish café in the limo. Charlie watched the long white limo pull up outside, taking up two and a half car spaces. Harry jumped outside and walked into the café in a perky fashion leaving Jimmy, the driver, who also drove the bus, in the car.

'Hay Harry, where you get that piece of shit from?' yelled Charlie. 'Move it out of the front of my shop.'

Harry laughed, pinched a chip from the behind the counter and slapped a couple of tickets by the cash register. 'Give me some fish,' he said, 'and I'll think about it.'

CHAPTER SIXTEEN

For months, Sheryl had dreamed of this moment; she had fantasized over and over again, and always in her dreams she had this seat. She sat spellbound as each wrestler paraded down the aisle to the tune of a deafening fanfare. Her stomach leaped into summersaults as they stood nearby, yelling into a microphone until their voices were hoarse. She was so close to the ring she could hear each grunt. So close she could see the ripple of muscles and the spray of sweat after each fall. She watched, too inspired for words as large men crashed to the floor and heaved themselves up again, and she told herself nothing could be better than this.

Steven was not so impressed.

He had sat through an hour and ten minutes of men dressed in every colour under the rainbow. He had seen men fly from the top of a cage and land on a rubbish truck or 'Pushed to the edge of existence', as one commentator put it. He watched as a man not five feet from him was thrown into a coffin, which was then set alight by his opponent's manager. With all the flare of a gothic magician, the small fat manager strutted and puffed with his torch, the audience screamed, some children cried and the commentator called it entertainment.

He watched a group of men enter on skateboards with trousers so baggy you could swing a cat in them. He watched as scantily-clad Brazilian women entered the ring behind a steel drum band, and he wondered what connection Brazil had with Jamaica.

He had seen Martin Latino 'Pile Drive', sending the women behind him into a frenzy.

He had seen a wrestler called 'Mongoose' pull a snake out of a black bag; wave it about the audience a bit before tormenting his opponent with it. He had managed to sit through an eight-man tag team match called, 'The combat of injustice', which as one of the commentators put it, 'crossed the sacred line of justice'.

All this was accompanied by the howls and screams of the women behind as they called the wrestlers things that he was sure were physically impossible. Their language made Beatrice's 'earthy talk' sound like something out of a fairy tale book.

The only good thing about all this was sitting next to Sheryl, hoping one day that he could arouse in her the passion he now saw on her face; that he could make her round chest heave with such anticipation as it was now doing at the thought of Johnston entering the ring.

He sighed and offered Sheryl a chocolate.

As much as Steven hated it, Beatrice loved it. She got her first autograph from Uno Sumo. His main winning move was to sit on his opponents from a great height, which was then repeated at least a dozen times in slow motion on the large TV screen on the walls of the arena.

Uno Sumo entered the arena dressed in an elaborate G-string with tassels. Watched by thousands under the lights of the auditorium, his extra large rump wobbled with each step as the tassels swung from side to side. Women cooed as he wiggled his arse like a Hawaiian.

'Agile isn't he?' said someone.

Others sighed.

Uno Sumo moved from one corner to another with a seductive swirl of his hips.

'Don't you just adore round men?' cooed one woman.

'OOOh, I love YOU,' shouted another.

'Shift your sweet arse over here, honey!'

'Baby, give me some.'

'Uno Sumo' smiled as another hand slapped his rump, he refused a microphone and then climbed up onto the ring and sat on his opponent.

One hour and twenty minutes of wrestling, thought Steven, *of men and woman throwing each other around the ring for nothing more than a large belt.* And now he was standing waiting, like the rest of them, for Johnston and Steel Ice to parade through the smoky doors and beat each other into oblivion.

'Mad Brady', the younger of the two commentators turned to Nefertiti and winked, 'My money is on Johnston,' he said.

Steel Ice appeared wearing a blue and red kilt and matching sash across his shoulders. He entered to the rhythms of Celtic drums and a smoke machine working overtime.

Sheryl's heart raced like the clappers.

'What's Steel playing at?' said Mad Brady into his microphone.

'Who knows,' said Frank. 'It was only last week in Spain he came dressed as a bullfighter claiming some past tie to Picasso.'

'I thought he was French?'

'Who, Steel?' said Frank.

'No Picasso,' Mad Brady laughed. 'Wasn't he French?'

'All I know,' said Frank with little enthusiasm, 'is Steel Ice is a man with a mission.'

'A man high on the smell of success,' Mad Brady added. 'He's looking mean as hell tonight.'

'Hmm...' Frank looked at his watch.

'The JR of wrestling!'

Frank looked at Brady.

'We are looking at a cataclysm of major proportion tonight,' Mad Brady yelled into his microphone. 'I don't envy Johnston.'

'Neither do I!' said Frank. 'What the hell does Big Sal know about managing?'

'Just look at him... if revenge is his weapon, he's more loaded than Robo Cop.'

With hands on his hips, he swaggered down the aisle, the screaming almost drowning out the 'Celtic Drums'.

Stepping on to the ring like a royal, he grabbed a microphone and began talking about his newly-discovered Scottish roots.

'All my life I have been a hard core wrestler!' he said 'With one eye on the ring and one over my shoulder, I have fought the best and beat them all.'

'You a true Scot?' yelled someone.

'Oooh, I love a man in a kilt.'

Steven heard it all and wondered what it was with women; give them a tight butt and a torso with more six packs than an off licence and suddenly they were talking like someone out of 'Loaded', or worse still, 'Cosmopolitan'.

'And now as I look deep into my soul,' Steel began to increase the volume in his voice, 'discovering the roots...'

'What the hell is he talking about? What roots is that?' said Frank. 'Get a decent hairdresser, luv!'

'I HAVE FOUND A PURPOSE!' Steel yelled. And with the agility of a lap dancer, he began to strip off his sash and kilt, ending with a few robust pelvic thrusts.

Steven choked on the last of his chocolates as some of the women behind sighed.

Sheryl stood up and stared into the entrance. More smoke filled the doorway accompanied by a couple of explosions.

'The audience is electric with excitement!' yelled Mad Brady.

As the smoke cleared away, the blonde, or 'Miss Whiplash', as Steven liked to call her, stood in the entrance with her whip held across her thigh.

The American flag appeared from the ceiling, slowly unfolding along with a few trapeze artists, who skimmed down from the ceiling twirling like butterflies on a wire.

Americans, thought Steven, as Johnston's tune belted out over the cheer of the crowds

'And here she is now, Big Sal,' said Mad Brady. 'Do you know why they call her 'Big Sal'?'

Frank sighed.

'It's because she a big-hearted gal,' laughed Mad Brady.

The crowd roared again as Big Sal walked down the aisle welding her whip in the air. Johnston's entrance music continued as his dark silhouette appeared from the smoke. Screams and yells filled the stadium, as knickers began to fall on the entranceway like a multi-coloured carpet for Johnston to walk on. Sheryl's heart pounded almost up to her throat. He tuned his back to the audience and flexed his arms, his back expanded as drops of water dribbled down his smooth skin. He shook his hair, then turned to face his audience and flexed his arms again.

139

Johnston stopped at Sheryl's corner, and she stared at his chest; she was close enough to see the tattoo around his nipple. She looked at his thick thighs and the chocolate-coloured skin sculptured across the line of his muscles. She could see each droplet of water that ran down his oiled chest, his white teeth as he grimaced, and his square hands clenching and unclenching by his side.

Nefertiti watched not in awe, but in silence for she had to belly dance in front of all these men without her Rodger nearby. How could she muster any passion for dancing when she missed his bugle? If only he had asked her about the paintings, if only he was into landscapes.

'More animal than man,' yelled Mad Brady, 'just look at him, the adrenaline pumping through his veins...' Brady took a breath. 'Two giants of men... two finely tuned athletics, who have a history behind them that's deeper than the Grand Canyon. Yes, you can cut the atmosphere with a knife here tonight. These two men have mortgaged their youth in pursuit of excellence, who is going to beat who? That's the question on everyone's lips!'

Frank looked at his colleague,

'It's going to be one hell of a dust up!' continued Mad Brady, his voice becoming shrill. 'Who will become the greatest of all time? What do you think?' said Mad Brady, turning to Beatrice with a microphone.

'OOOH yeah!' she yelled.

Johnston grabbed a microphone from Frank.

'You are a joke, man,' he yelled. 'There is more Scottish blood in my mother's box of shortbread than in your fat arse!'

Steel Ice ran to the edge of the ring, dramatically leaning over the ropes. 'You don't call the shots around here, I do.' He shook his fist at

Johnston. 'By the time I'm finished with you, Sal won't have anything to manage.' He glared at his ex wife, before pacing about the ring like a cornered polecat.

But Sheryl didn't catch a word, she was too busy wondering how much taller Johnston was to her, and if she stood beside him, where her lips would be…

Steel Ice mouthed some obscenities and gave the finger to Johnston.

'I am gonna whip your arse, man!' yelled Johnston, as the crowd cheered.

Johnston then dropped his microphone, ran to the ringside, threw himself under the rope and rolled onto the ring, whereby Steel Ice began to kick into him, not leaving a mark.

Steven smiled.

****

Rodger listened for as long as possible then offered Bert a proposition, a proposition that Bert jumped at. Bert handed Rodger the costume, zipped him up when required and watched (keeping his opinions to himself) as Rodger strapped on his bugle's hat over the top of the costume. He led Rodger to the platforms near the ceiling, strapped him into his harness and wished him luck with his woman. Then with two cheques, one from Rodger and one from the Wrestling Federation, Bert walked back to the hotel to watch the football.

****

Johnston picked Steel up and then after a dramatic pause, threw Steel head first onto the metallic steps going up onto the ring. A hollow crunch echoed through the hall, Steven winced, Beatrice cheered, and Sheryl sighed.

Nefertiti wasn't even watching, she had taken up her predancing meditation pose and was trying to erase the thoughts of rich coffee, chilled chardonnay and chocolates, all served by Rodger in his bugle's hat. Rodger had stirred a passion in her soul she never knew existed. Why could he not just paint flowers like everyone else?

'Oooo, that's gotta hurt,' said Frank over the blast of trumpets and drums.

A wrestler dressed as a gladiator appeared on the scene with a woman beside him, who wore some sort of Stone Age cave woman outfit. With arms like dumb bells, and her modesty protected by a few small bits of fur, she ran alongside the gladiator.

'Here we go again,' said Frank.

Steven watched on in amazement, as the Rachel Welsh look-alike managed to run with her modesty just covered.

'Look who is coming now...Gladiator!' yelled Mad Brady, whose voice was now higher than a choirboy's. 'And he wants blood; Johnston's!'

'Watch out, Johnston!' Beatrice yelled.

'What will they think of next?' muttered Frank.

'I wouldn't be in Johnston's shoes for anything,' continued Mad Brady.

'This business has gone crazy,' Frank moaned.

'Gladiator is going to go for the kill,' screeched Mad Brady.

'In my day, wrestler were men in black tights.'

'But we didn't have women like that, did we?' said Mad Brady, 'thank goodness for silicone and Lycra!' he yelled into the microphone, pumping a fist into the air.

'YEHAAAA,' yelled Beatrice pumping her fist into the air.

Whiplash grabbed the Stone Age woman by the hair; the referee tried to stop them as they fell to the ground and rolled around a bit. Steven, like many of the other males, was looking on, wondering how securely attached the fur was.

Then Rodger chose his moment, dressed in a fully padded panda suit, he abseiled down the middle of the hall mastering a few little twirls as he went.

'What the hell is that?' asked Mad Brady.

Nefertiti looked up. 'Oh my God,' she said. 'He's wearing the bugle's hat.'

****

Conway and Martin pulled into the Corran Halls and parked in a disabled car park. Conway checked his sticker then jumped out of the car. Martin was already out of the car and checking his BMW parked by the bus.

'If that bastard's done anything to my BMW,' said Martin, pulling out his spare set of keys. 'I'll swing for him.'

Conway, using his policeman mentality, searched the car for clues and came across a note book in the back seat. He read some mumblings about the bugle and his love for the Flower of Scotland, and decided that Rodger was more of a loony than he and Martin had first thought.

'Sick bastard,' said Conway. 'Come on, he must be inside.'

The two men ran to the entrance, Conway threw a couple of Rennies in his mouth and flashed his card at an American bouncer. The bouncer looked at the card and figured Paisley must be somewhere close, and let them in.

Martin and Conway raced into the hall as the panda was acrobatically descending from above. They watched as he landed on top of Johnston, who was standing outside the ring near Steven.

'A panda in wrestling, who'd have thought it?' said Conway.

'A panda with a codpiece, who've have thought of that?' asked Martin.

'Americans,' said Conway, with a large trumpet-like belch.

Martin said nothing, but nodded with a 'You said it' look on his face.

CHAPTER SEVENTEEN

Sheryl looked out the limousine window and sighed for the fifth time in as many minutes. Typically, her mother was having a whale of a time spread out on the plush seats with a smirk that needed slapping, while Sheryl sat hunched under Harry's coat. She cursed herself for expecting the impossible; that nothing would go wrong; what a fool she was.

Sheryl had allowed herself to enjoy every moment of the evening. She had shared in the passion and drama of it all, until the gods of fate, Karma, call it what you will had got the final laugh.

'It's not that bad!' said Beatrice, with little feeling. 'Look at Rodger, he's putting on a brave face.'

Rodger said nothing; he was still in his panda suit with the panda head on his lap, and his precious bugle hat inside it. He looked beseechingly at Nefertiti, but she was in her meditating pose with her eyes shut.

'In front of all those people, and all those wrestlers.'

'I don't see why you're so bothered. It's not as if you ever bothered about your appearance before!' said Beatrice.

'Today would have to be one of the most embarrassing days of my life. This was supposed to be my weekend, and you,' snapped Sheryl, 'have managed to spoil it every inch of the way!'

'I think you managed most of that yourself. After all, it was you who was too pissed to drive. And it was you who wore those awful grey knickers.'

'Some people like sensible underpants,' mumbled Steven.

145

'Absolutely,' said Harry.

'Maybe you should think 'bout buying decent underwear,' Rodger muttered. Sheryl crossed her arms and huffed a bit, these days she hardly ever thought about nice underwear. 'It always worked for my Nefertiti.'

Nefertiti opened her eyes, 'What were you thinking of? First me Flower of Scotland and then ...' she looked at the bugle's hat. 'Why don't you just video us doing it.'

'I thought if you just saw our bugle's hat dancing in the air, and no one else would know like...cause I was in disguise ...you always liked me dancing with it.'

'Me 'eart is wretched,' muttered Nefertiti with a dramatic gesture.

Beatrice looked at Sheryl. 'Just 'cause you're on the shelf,' she said, 'it doesn't mean you have to let yourself go, does it?'

That bloody shelf, thought Sheryl, if she had heard it once she had heard countless time, she looked at her mother and wondered how many ways you could ram a shelf into her thin lips.

'Me heart is broken in to a million pieces, 'ow can I go on?' sighed Nefertiti.

'For God's sake, Naf-arse, give it a break. How many men would abseil in a panda suit with a codpiece strapped to them just for love?' snapped Beatrice.

'What do you mean?'

'Look at Sheryl,' said Beatrice. 'The only thing she could pull was a married man, a part-time lover who hid his car around the corner.'

'Thanks Mum.'

'Rodger's a real catch compared to him, and he doesn't drink.'

Rodger was not only a sober man, he was also quite an agile man. In a previous life, so he told many, he was an acrobat for a Russian circus.

****

Rodger had stood on the ledge waiting for the right moment to descend and tempt his Egyptian princess. He had made friends with the technicians; he had paid them money to do what he asked, all he needed now was his plan to unfold nicely. Under the heat of the lights, he closed his eyes and inhaled in his past. After a few deep breaths and a small amount of chanting, Rodger was ready. *Nefertiti, you are mine*, he whispered more than once, then he opened his eyes.

He looked down at his audience, his aim was good and with a nod to the technicians, the panda began to make his descent.

No one noticed the panda at first. His round black and white body was just a pimple in the distance as Steel and Johnston thrashed it out in the ring.

Johnston picked Steel up and threw him against the metal steps, the crowd hushed as the noise of the crash filled the hall. Then the Proclaimers began to sing as the panda began to twirl and the gold straps of the codpiece caught the light. By the time he was half-way down, some of the children started to notice and some began to point.

Rodger, however, knew the exact moment when Nefertiti saw him and that's when he opened his legs in a V-like position and the concertina codpiece sprang forth like a jack in the box, bobbing up and down with each movement.

'Jess Brady, will you look at that!' said Frank.

Some of the adults tried to cover the children's eyes.

The codpiece was studded with green and red baubles. At the tip was a red gem the size of a tennis ball, which pulsated in time to the music.

The panda perfected a few pelvic thrusts as the jewelled member bounced from one knee to another, and soon no one was watching the wrestlers at all. Instead, the crowd was fixated on the codpiece swaying between the panda's legs, rhythmically in time to the Proclaimers now playing:

When ye go will ye send back a letter from America

Take a look at the rail track

Some of the crowd smiled, others laughed and cheered, some even clapped.

Bathgate no more, Lochaber no more

He twirled closer to the ground, mesmerising the crowd as his codpiece swayed like a jewelled palm tree, getting bigger and bigger.

'Be still me 'eart,' muttered Nefertiti. 'There is more than one of 'em.'

Johnston said nothing, he stepped off the ring and moved beside where Steven was sitting for a better view.

Mad Brady and Frank said nothing either, what could they say? No one had told them about the panda wearing a codpiece, and neither of them had ever heard of the Proclaimers.

The panda looked at his audience, he had his Egyptian princess's complete attention. He stopped for minute as the Proclaimers faded out then, directing his swing towards Nefertiti, he began to recite his poem to the tune of one of Nefertiti's favourite songs, while gesturing like a very bad Shakespearian actor.

OH NEFERTITI, MY BUGLE IS CALLING, CALLING YOU.

FROM EAST TO WEST IT WILL NOT REST, TILL YOU ARE NEAR.

*IT WANTS YOUR FLOWER OF SCOTLAND TO UNVEIL ITS LOVE
TO ME.
OH MY NEFERTITI, COME BACK, COME BACK TO ME.*

Nefertiti stared at the panda as he swung closer to her. She knew
that voice, she knew that song, she knew that bloody codpiece; what
the hell was he doing? She watched the panda twirl like a pendulum as
a whole gamut of emotions began to churn in her stomach.

The panda was now in full flight, he had the whole audience
including his Nefertiti in the palm of his paw, or so he thought. So the
panda went for a somersault just to add a bit of panache, a sort of full
stop to his poem. But the panda was not as agile as he used to be, and
with a very high-pitched, *You have my heart now take the rest of me,*
the panda lost control and sped to the ground, landing on top of
Johnston.

'Oh bugger,' echoed Rodger's voice into the microphone.

Johnston said more than that, but luckily no one heard.

CHAPTER EIGHTEEN

Nefertiti had stared at the wide screens on the walls as they repeatedly flashed the fall of the panda onto Johnston. The whole gamut of emotions that had been churning in her stomach now began to churn into one big ball of anger. *Everyone has seen it*, she thought, *the whole bleeding world has just seen the bugle's hat; my bugle's hat, not only is my Flower of Scotland public property, but the bugle's hat is on film forever.* She quickly scanned the hall and her eyes stopped at the ring. Sitting in the corner was big Sal's whip. *Retribution,* she thought, *sweet retribution.*

'Of all my years in wrestling,' muttered Frank 'I can't believe what we just saw.'

Johnston, laying flat on his back with a dazed 'What the hell is going on' look, couldn't either. He turned to Steven and saw a sweet, willing man who was just the age he liked. 'Help me,' he said.

Sheryl, standing next to Steven, assumed he meant both of them, and for a moment, thought about kissing the panda but instead, with Steven's help, rolled the mumbling panda over onto his back and helped Johnston up.

Nefertiti, with the swift movement of an agile mature woman, jumped onto the stage, and with a lot of shouting, grabbed Big Sal's whip. 'Retribution is mine,' she yelled, and with an athletic swing that came from years of dancing with a cane, she began to taunt the Panda. It was an impressive performance, impressive enough to whip the audience up into frenzy, and cause the majority of men to look at the more mature women in a new light.

150

'Look at that, Frank, I reckon we've found the infamous Nefertiti,' said Mad Brady.

Frank said nothing; a whip-wielding granny was not what he called entertainment, let alone wrestling.

****

Steven looked out the window of the limo and ventured a comment. 'It could be worse,' he said.

'How?

'Come on, Sheryl, don't be SO melodramatic.' Beatrice sniffed. 'They're just wrestlers'.

'And some of 'em are complete arseholes,' said Jimmy. But Sheryl didn't see it that way. In her eyes, her afternoon had been ruined, and it all was thanks to Beatrice and her stupid wheelchair.

****

Beatrice had been parked at the front of the aisle, just close enough to feel the wind of the whip, and eventually just close enough for the whip to catch into the spokes of the wheel. And when Beatrice tried to accelerate away, the whip wound itself further in.

Nefertiti let go of the whip as she began to chase the panda down the aisle, with the crowd laughing and cheering in the background.

'What the hell's happening?' Beatrice yelled at Sheryl. Sheryl said nothing, but bent over the wheel of the chair to untangle the whip. She didn't see Steven at the control of the chair, or her skirt dangle into the spokes of the wheel.

Steven, a little panicky, pressed the controls. The chair lurched into reverse, taking Sheryl's skirt with it, and more of the whip.

The crowd was silenced as Mad Brady made to speak again. The next thing Sheryl heard was a rip, followed by a cold chill at the side of her leg. Sheryl looked down to see the gradual unveiling of her underwear take place, and realised that the worse nightmare that could ever happen was now happening to her, and it was being filmed on the wide screen on the walls. Of all the days she had picked to wear her worse grey knickers, it had to be today.

****

'You and your bloody wheelchair,' muttered Sheryl, while staring out of the limo's window; this time no one said anything.

****

Conway and Martin had watched the whole thing.

'That's Rodger,' said Martin.

'What the hell is he doing in a panda suit?' Conway fumed.

They ran to the dressing room, but were stopped by the bouncers. They tried to run to the exit and were held up by the audience. Finally, they made it outside only to see the panda and Nefertiti getting into the white limo.

Conway jumped into his car and began to follow.

Martin jumped into his and began to think.

CHAPTER NINETEEN

Sheryl, Beatrice and Nefertiti were all sulking in silence as the limo drove up the hill behind Oban, Jimmy noticed the fiesta was still behind them. He drummed his fingers on the steering wheel.

'We're being followed,' he said.

'Who would want to follow us?' mumbled Steven.

Rodger, with his eyes still closed, could only guess. He muttered something about ignoring.

Nefertiti let out a dramatic sigh, 'For God's sake,' she snapped, but no one listened. Jimmy had turned up the speed, he had plans; plans that involved the young waitress sitting beside him, plans that involved really impressing her.

With a loud screech, he changed direction and headed back out of Oban toward the turn off to Connel.

'Don't do ignoring,' he said with a side glance at the waitress, and then overtook a lorry.

****

Conway watching the limo change direction and he spat the remains of a cigarette out of the window.

'All right, you asked for it,' he said, with a prolonged belch then pressed on the accelerator. The back seat slid forward, thumping into the back of Conway's seat. Conway didn't even notice, all his attention was focused ahead on the white limo and the 'bastard' that was in it.

****

Harry, intent on getting a party going, pulled out a couple of cans

153

of beer and a selection of crisps.

'Export anyone?' he said.

Jimmy sped around a bend as Harry pulled the can open, beer frothed over the rim and dribbled onto the floor.

'Bugger,' said Harry.

Sheryl, who was trying to keep her dignity with a coat that refused to stay shut, stared out the window, while Steven stared in the other direction, he had had enough.

'I think I've lost him,' said Jimmy over his shoulder.

But the fiesta followed, easing its way through the traffic like a slick operator.

'If this is your doing, Rodger?' said Nefertiti 'If it's anything to do with them paintings, I swear I will not be responsible for me actions.'

Beatrice sat back with a quiet smile; *at last a man who enjoys speed,* she thought, *a man who can take a corner, a man who can take a wheel and make it his.* She pulled out her flask and took a huge swig, she was going to enjoy every damn moment.

'The fiesta's still there,' said Jimmy, throwing a look at the waitress, she smiled wanly back at him.

Harry took a sip of his can then offered some to Steven. He turned to Rodger, who was now staring out the back window, and tapped his shoulder, Rodger jumped, knocking the can, and beer poured onto Harry's lap and down his leg.

'Bugger,' he said again.

Jimmy made to do a right turn, he indicated and at the last moment, did a u-turn back down the road, the fiesta tried to follow and collided into the back of a lorry full of frozen fish.

As Conway got out the car, Jimmy turned back, drove past, tooted his horn and then gave the finger to Conway.

'Was all that necessary?' asked Harry, brushing his trousers.

'Absolutely,'' snapped Jimmy. 'No one takes the piss out of my driving.'

****

Conway sat on the pavement, turning his police badge between his fingers, blocking his view was the lorry driver swearing at him in Gaelic, and using gestures that required no translation. With his third fag in as many minutes, the driver pointed to the fiesta, now buckling under the weight of frozen fish.

Conway said nothing, his mind was on bigger things.

Somehow he had to get back to O'Leary's Oyster Bar, somehow he had to get that bastard alone; perhaps a disguise he thought, take Mr. Brassiere by surprise.

Conway; oblivious to the cats beginning to collect around his car, pulled a box of papers from the back seat, tossed aside a few bits of cod, took what he needed and began looking for a lift.

****

Steven let out a long sigh and watched as they headed back into Oban. By the time they had passed the Corran Halls, he had made a decision.

'Let me out,' he snapped.

'What?'

'I said let me out, I've had enough.'

'Come on Steven, the party's just starting.'

'I said stop this damn car!'

Beatrice pulled a 'Do something or at least say something' look at Sheryl. But Sheryl, with a few tuts, looked back out the window.

'Steven,' Beatrice finally piped up. 'The worst is over...'

'Pull over here,' snapped Steven.

With a shrug and a 'Who's rattled his cage' look, Jimmy stopped the car just outside the backpacker hostel.

'Stay for a can,' said Harry, still keen on the idea of a pre-reception party.

Steven grabbed his coat.

'At least take Sheryl's phone then,' said Beatrice.

Steven slid the phone into his pocket and, with a final glare, left.

'There goes your last chance,' muttered Beatrice under her breath.

Sheryl pretended not to hear.

****

Martin drove into the private car space just behind the 'Wee Bit of Art' shop. The gathering was in full swing and Status Quo, which had been on repeat for the last two hours, had finally been changed to a more subtle choice of music. Blasting from the back door of the gallery was the Songs of Solomon, unrecognised and not particularly liked by Martin. He stepped out of his car with the now familiar stabbing feeling in his stomach, and raced towards the gallery.

Chubby had been busy; she had called every woman she knew.

'There's wine and chocolates,' she said, 'and there's something here that once you've seen, you'll never be the same again.'

Many came, Chubby was well-liked, the type who if she said there were chocolates and wine, then there would be enough to feed an army. Plus she had good taste.

Martin opened the door and stopped in his tracks. The gallery, his gallery was reeking of joss sticks and full of half-cut women munching chocolates and getting in touch with their 'inner Goddess'.

'What the hell is gong on?' he yelled, but no one heard.

He stared into the joss stick fog; he had never seen so many women looking so content.

> *The joints of thy thighs are like jewels*
> *Thy navel is like a round goblet which*
> *wantedth not liquor*

'Imogene?'

Still no one noticed; they were all looking at Chubby standing on a beanbag, swaying to the music.

'Now you see the truth,' she said, with a wave of pink sparkling. 'Now you see the miracle that is woman.'

'And why men watch porn,' said another.

Martin was beginning to feel like an intruder, a foreigner, in his own shop.

He stared harder into the fog; just below Chubby on the floor, staring with rapt concentration was his little Haystack.

> *Thy breast like two young rose*
> *The roof of they mouth like the best wine*
> *Go down sweet lady*

'Imogene, what the hell is going on?'

But Imogene didn't hear, she was experiencing a transformation, she was experiencing a rebirth of emotion. She was discovering the goddess within, and she hadn't felt sick once! She was looking at things differently; her pregnancy was no longer an inconvenience of heartburn and swelling feet. Her pregnancy was a miracle, a miracle of womanhood, a miracle which she now wanted to share with her

157

newfound sisters..

She looked up at Chubby. 'You have changed my life, so you have.'

Chubby patted her arm with a serene smile.

Martin looked around, and for the first time, saw Rodger's paintings; Martin was almost moved. He poured himself a glass of wine and then with half a strawberry cream in his mouth, a thought came to him. What if Nefertiti were to see these paintings? She would be moved as he almost was? Not only would the 'Rodger' problem be solved, but maybe more. If Ole Nef can sell belly dancing at her time of life, then maybe she could sell abstract fannies. Besides, he thought he had heard her talk of the goddess within. She was actually quite convincing.

A quick glimpse of the art work, thought Martin, a few bottles of wine and bit of the old Martin patter and he could have the Queen of the Clyde eating out of his hands, and more to the point, eating out of Rodger's.

'Chubby?' he said. 'Where're the wrestlers holding their reception?'

CHAPTER TWENTY

The limo parked outside the Lochfeta Boarding House, and in silence, the women got out. Rodger, uninvited, followed hoping for a chance to explain, a chance to win Nefertiti around, and hopefully a bed for the night. He pulled the wheelchair from the boot and helped Beatrice in.

Rona saw the limo from her lounge, 'Here they come,' she said to Eric and raced to the front door. Sheryl didn't even have a chance to knock.

Rona opened the door looking for gossip about beefy wrestlers and belly dancing, and came across Sheryl mournfully standing in an overcoat, and a grim-looking Nefertiti tapping half a whip against her thigh. Rona was just about to say, 'Come in,' when Beatrice pushed her way through on a screeching wheelchair, with bits of Sheryl's skirt and the rest of the whip whirling around on her wheel.

Rona said nothing, instead she walked to the kitchen, put the kettle on and handed a plate of Jaffa cakes to Eric.

'This'll be good,' she said.

Eric wasn't so sure, and he certainly didn't care, it was Saturday night, his Karaoke night. *One hour,* he told himself as he walked into the musty living room with the Jaffa cakes, *one hour and I'll be off.*

Nefertiti screwed up her nose, she needed something more than tea. Something stronger, something in a matching cup and saucer and without the remains of its last contents stained in a dribble on the outside. She watched Sheryl demolish hers and took a tentative sip.

'You only have to face 'em,' said Rona. 'Just remember, today's grey kickers is tomorrow's laundry.'

'At least it was only your bleeding knickers they saw,' muttered Nefertiti.

Sheryl said nothing. Nefertiti in a sour mood was not a pleasant sight, and neither was her mother. Beatrice was rustling in the next room; it was the sort of rustle that involved whisky and a fair amount of anger.

Beatrice was consoling herself to the fact that tonight, her big night for meeting the wrestlers would be done in a wheelchair that was stuck in first gear, and screeched into action like a cat having its tail cut.

The gearbox, according to Sheryl was jammed, and the parts for a new one were at home. Beatrice drained her glass and phoned George.

Rona watched Sheryl tuck into her third Jaffa cake. 'Maybe I can help,' she said. 'I've still got some clothes I used to wear before I joined Slimming World.'

Nefertiti pulled a face, (which no one noticed), Rona was a trim woman in her late forties, wearing white three quarter leg trousers, (a size too small) white high heel sandals, red toenails, and a black tee shirt with *don't stop me now* splashed across her chest in sequins. She had a fag in one hand, sights of Oban tea towel in the other, and a way of standing that demanded attention. This was a woman who dressed from Tesco's and was proud of it, a woman who knew most of the other shoppers in Tesco's and was proud of it, and a woman whose idea of a good night out was Karaoke at Clara's followed by a curry and a snog (in no particular order). How was she going to help someone like Sheryl?

Nefertiti followed Sheryl and Rona into Rona's bedroom, expecting little more than a room in the same state as her teacup.

Nefertiti was taken aback. The room was fragrant free and tidy, with mirrored wardrobes full of clothes that definitely didn't come from Tesco's.

It turned out Rona liked fantasies of an erotic nature, and she made a small living selling these fantasies to poor lonely souls just like Sheryl. Her wardrobe was full of leather bodices, and velvet outfits for all sizes.

'You may find this hard to believe, Sheryl, but I could make you look like a woman a man would want to shag,' said Rona, 'even Steven.'

Eric said nothing; he had witnessed many of Rona's attempts. Rona was as tactless as a comedian desperate for fame. He cleared away the teapot and offered Rodger the last of the biscuits. 'Fancy a pint?' he said.

Rodger looked towards Rona's bedroom.

'On you go,' yelled Rona. 'And see if you can find Steven while you're at it.'

'Come on,' said Eric, 'before she changes her mind.'

And this time, Rodger followed.

****

Sheryl stood in front of the mirror tugging at her grey knickers, with her bosom swinging in a bra that Rona wouldn't even use for a sling shot. Rona pulled a black leather corset out of the cupboard. Rona had visions of Sheryl in something eastern and black with her huge bosom wobbling over the top like jelly.

'This'll get em drooling,' she said. 'And it'll take the attention away from your hips.'

'Not every woman likes to put it on a plate,' yelled Beatrice, who was still downstairs and feeling left out. 'Some men like to do a little unwrapping themselves.'

Rona pulled the bra off and tossed it in the bin and then proceeded to try wrapping something half the size of Sheryl around her. Sheryl watched in the mirror like a four-year being dressed by an overbearing adult, as Rona tried to close the six-inch gap at the back.

****

Eric and Rodger walked in to Clara's pub and peered into the smoky atmosphere. On the scratched dance floor moving to a toothless man singing Hero was a couple oblivious to the no-smoking rule.

Steven was sitting on a stool talking to a weary-looking barman and a woman with a slightly askew wig, and matchstick legs, who everyone knew as Nellie.

'I loved her from the first time I saw her,' said Steven. 'She looked miserable and it became my mission.'

'What?' said Nellie, exposing a set of loose fitting dentures.

'To make her smile!'

'Ooooh, I see.'

'And she hardly notices me. I give up,' he said, tossing a pork scratching into his mouth and missing it.

'Give up what?' said Nellie.

'She said 'treat 'em mean, keep 'em keen',' said Steven.

'Who?'

'Beatrice! Mind, Nefertiti's advice is far more intelleeeectual.'

'Nefertiti?'

'She says I'm to look at her like she is the only woman I ever wanted to bed, while telling her how interesting she is.'

'In short, look at their tits and listen,' said the barman.

'Oooh, how wonderful,' said Nellie. 'Pretending you're interested, can you do that?'

'Sheryl is interesting,' said Steven, with a swing of his Babycham bottle. He took a final gulp from his drink and began to ponder his novel.

Porter's heart was broken.

He watched Sheryl push a glass across the bar, and with a rustle of nylon, move to the next cowboy. Her scent lingered and Porter, for a moment, was lost in the past to a time when that scent lingered on his sheets.

He stared at her shapely hips and wondered about the pistol strapped beneath the skirt.

But Big John was back on the scene and Big John was all she talked about.

Porter downed his whisky and stood up from the bar. He had work to do, a mission to complete and once that was done, the truth about Big John would come out and maybe, just maybe...

Eric tapped Steven on the shoulder.

Steven jumped.

'What you doing here?' said Eric.

'Talking piss,' said the barman.

'About some girl,' said Nellie.

'And a guy called Porter.'

'I thought there was code of confidential...lity...' said Steven, 'among barmen.'

'That'll be for a paying customer,' said the barman.

'OH!' slurred Steven. 'Forgot, no money left.'

'Let's get you home,' muttered Rodger.

163

'About bloody time,' said the barman. 'He has been singing like a prick for the last two hours.'

'What is it a woman wants?'

'Yeah the eternal questions, Steven, now bugger off, before I do something you'll regret,' said the barman.

'Regrets, I've had a few,' sang Steven, looking into Nellie's eyes,

'I did it MYYY WAY,' she yelled back.

Steven lent back, mis-calculated the bar and fell off the stool.

The barman raised his eye to the ceiling and was just about to say something about Steven's great pitch when Sheryl's mobile rang.

Rodger pulled it out of Steven's pocket and answered it.

'Sheryl, is that you?' came the reply.

'MARTIN?' said Rodger. 'Is that you? You have ruined my life.'

'Oh, Sheryl, where is she? No, wait a minute. Rodger, is that you? I think I can save it,' yelled Martin.

'Is it that bastard Martin?' said Steven, sitting up with a flash before falling back down again.

'It?' said Rodger.

'Your life, your paintings,' continued Martin. 'Women loved them. I have a group here just now getting in touch with the Goddess within. We got to get Nefertiti to see them. We could make a frigging fortune.'

'It's Martin, isn't it?' Steven sat up again. 'She's no cleaner, you know!' he yelled into an imaginary phone, and then looked up at Nellie 'She's too good for him.'

****

Eric and Rodger took Steven out of the bar and tried to steer him into the direction of Lochfeta. But Steven would have none of it. Once he heard that Martin was going to O'Leary's Oyster Bar, Steven decided to follow.

'There are scores needin to be settled,' he yelled in the street. 'And I, Steven, am gonna do what Porter would have done!'

'Break a leg, Stevie,' yelled Nellie, while waving a fag in the drizzle.

Steven, with a stagger, waved back then placed his arms around both men and crossed the street. He had his pals and Sheryl's mobile, all he needed now was to find out just exactly where this Oyster bar was.

****

George put the phone down and grinned. It was the sort of grin Morag had seen before.

'That'll be herself then?' she said.

George handed Morag a Bombay Gin and poured himself a Royal Blacker.

'You'll be seeing her later, I suppose?' said Morag, with a bored expression.

'Hmm, I'm going to take my time, her car exploded you know.'

'Don't they always.'

'And her wheelchair's not too hot either. Apparently, it squeals like a cat with its tail caught in a gin trap.'

Morag watched George pull her husband's wheelchair from the cupboard, and with a tuneless whistle, he begin to dust it down.

'I take it she'll not know you'll be coming.'

'No.'

'And you're going to surprise her, with that?'

'Yep.'

George pulled out a can of WD40 and Morag's patience dwindled.

'There'll be nothing wrong with that chair; no one's touched it since my Jack died. Besides, you and fixing don't mix, you start tinkering with that chair, and it'll be in bits by the time my gin is finished.'

George sat in the chair and gave it a test run up the hall.

'Don't know why you bother, look at how she treated Robert.'

'Some men like a little fire,' muttered George. 'Who wants an easy life?'

'You're just saying that 'cause you've never had to wake up to the same person raking over the same arguments for forty years,' said Morag. 'Staying married is hard work, I should know, I worked bloody hard at mine, but not half as hard as that poor Robert.'

George switched off at the "bloody hard" stage, he had heard it all before. *I'll book a taxi for nine,* he thought; *keep her waiting; that was the most important thing.*

****

It was Nefertiti who finally found an outfit for Sheryl that not only fitted her, but made looking in the mirror for Sheryl a pleasant experience. It was right at the back of the wardrobe and it was the colour that first caught Nefertiti's eye.

'Surprising enough, that looks good on you,' said Rona. She slipped a Paul Simon CD on and 'Twenty ways to leave your lover' began to play.

Sheryl stared at her reflection; even with an underwire bra making its presence felt, Sheryl felt pretty good, in fact she felt like she could face the world. The grey knickers were forgotten, the hangover was gone and she was going to see the wrestlers, she shimmied her breasts in front of the mirror and began to dance; in blue velvet, it felt fantastic.

'*Just slip out the back, Jack, make a new plan, Stan, don't need to be coy, Roy, just set your self free...*'

Sheryl circled her hips.

'For someone your size,' said Rona, 'you're quite light on your feet. I reckon you could be quite an inspiration to fat people.'

Nefertiti tutted, she had been saying that from the first time she saw Sheryl dance.

Beatrice looked at Sheryl's bag laying open on the floor, a piece of blue sequined material was hanging out. She pulled it out, unravelling Sheryl's costume. It was the sort of blue that made red hair stunning, and the sort of shape made for curves. Beatrice felt a lump in her throat, how could her daughter make something so beautiful?

Beatrice screeched in to the lounge to see her daughter dancing, and for a moment stopped and stared as she tried to adjust herself to the fact that her daughter looked attractive and could dance. In the mirror above the fireplace, Beatrice saw the reflection of her daughter; she saw a look she hadn't seen for years, a look of happiness. Beatrice forgot about her wheelchair, she forgot about the broken gearbox, all she thought about was how to keep that look on her daughter's face. Then Beatrice thought of Sheryl's costume, and before Sheryl had a chance to notice her mother's presence, Beatrice wheeled herself back into the bedroom and meticulously packed Sheryl's costume into her bag.

CHAPTER TWENTY-ONE

O'Leary's Oyster bar was situated in the reception room of the Columba Hotel, which was owned by a young dark man from Glasgow called Iain. Iain had been caught selling things he shouldn't be selling once too often by the police, and once too often his father had paid them off. Iain's father had had enough and bought a cheap rundown hotel (The Columbia) and with a small lump sum, set Iain a mission.

Iain took over the rundown Victorian building and was inspired. His first of many inspirations was the Oyster Bar. The second was getting involved with Harry, and the third was staying friendly with the local policemen, such as Cocolder.

Iain was waiting in the reception of the hotel for Cocolder to arrive, while Sheryl was making an entrance by the back door of the Columbia.

She had walked out of the Lochfeta B&B with a can of Red Bull, a packet of tic-tacs, and one of Rona's G-strings making its presence felt like a forgotten piece of toilet paper.

Sheryl had grand plans of staying sober. She had grand plans of being able to walk rather than stagger in her new velvet look, and she had grand plans of facing her humiliation with just a little bit of guts. She was hoping to wake up in the morning with no feelings of guilt or remorse; but instead with a clear head and a picture of her and Johnston in her camera, and the memory of that moment to match.

Sheryl popped a tic-tac in her mouth, stepped out of the limo and just missed a puddle.

A grumpy-looking cat stared up from a couple of wheelie bins a few feet away. It hissed, scowled then made his escape, sending some suspicious smelling plastic wrappers flying. Sheryl adjusted her G-string then pulled out her mother's wheelchair. She never even noticed the cat.

****

'This way,' said Harry and led them through the back door and into the kitchen. Beatrice's chair screeched into action as she tried to manoeuvre it through the slim doorway. After the third attempt, she made it through, knocking over whatever was in her way including a bunch of leeks hanging over the side of a bench.

'Watch me veg,' yelled Mohamed, a hot-looking chef. He was standing by the stove vigorously shaking a frying pan. He slid the contents of the frying pan on to two plates then barked at a waitress.

Standing by another bench sharpening his knife stood a small muscular man. He looked up from a row of gaping fish, saw Harry and smiled.

'Hey mate,' he yelled, with a casual wave of his knife.

'Why the hell are we coming through this way?' yelled Beatrice, knocking over some empty bottles.

Harry laughed, 'You're the surprise. Nobody knows you're coming, it was Chubby's idea!'

'Table number two finished,' yelled the waitress, coming back in, she gave Sheryl the once over and raced out with another two plates.

'These are the belly dancers,' said Harry to them all in the kitchen.

Nefertiti struck a half-hearted pose.

The chef laughed, waving his knife in the direction of Beatrice.

'You?'

Beatrice threw the chief her best 'What do you bloody think,' look while attempting a three-point turn.

The chef laughed again. 'Cause I have some drums and some pals, we could play for you.'

Harry's face lit up, 'See everything's gonna be fine.'

Beatrice had her doubts.

****

A taxi arrived at the front of The Columbia and Conway stepped out holding a brown paper bag. The taxi driver glanced at the old Victorian building, sprayed his car with air freshener and then drove off.

Conway looked down at his clothes and realised that he was conspicuous, and not to mention smelly. He needed to change, maybe even a disguise. The thought of a disguise excited him; he hadn't indulged for years. In his heyday, Conway had perfected many disguises, even a female hairdresser. Back then, he was known as the chameleon, the chameleon with good legs and not a bad pert walk. He looked down at his potbelly. *That was twenty years ago, at least,* he thought, could he still pull of a disguise?

Conway spied a round dark-haired girl jump out of a car and walk towards what he assumed was the staff entrance.

'Hey you,' he shouted, pulling out his badge. 'Fancy helping the police with a case?' When that didn't work, he offered her money.

****

Harry led Nefertiti to her dressing room, and Sheryl and Beatrice to O'Leary's Oyster Bar. It was full of wrestlers and various people, some of whom Sheryl recognised, including Mad Brady and Frank.

Mad Brady and Frank hadn't expected to see Sheryl again, especially looking attractive. No one did, and as she stood at the entrance, everyone stopped talking and stared. Sheryl took a deep breath, and walked in with a strut learnt in one of Nefertiti's classes.

Frank and Mad Brady watched the strut with admiration.

'She's got balls,' whispered Frank.

'The size of an elephant,' said Mad Brady.

Harry, with a twinkle in his eye, handed Sheryl a diet coke with ice and Beatrice a double whisky.

'This is Sheryl and Bea,' he said. 'Why don't you show 'em some good ole American hospitality?'

Mad Brady threw Frank a 'What, in a small rundown place like this,' look and pulled the first wrestler who walked by.

'Hey Mongoose, come and meet a nice Scotch gal,' he said.

Sheryl smiled as she was introduced to a softly-spoken German man, who was missing his pet snake. She smiled even more when she met the Crickey brothers and Martin Latino, a dark man in tight trousers who was about as Latin (to quote Harry) as a takeaway nacho.

'You know, Sheryl, wrestling aint what it's cracked up to be!' said Frank.

'Don't take any notice,' said Mad Brady. 'After a few beers, old tuna neck here starts to talk crazy.'

Beatrice let out a cackle. She was being entertained by a vanilla-scented Uno Sumo, who found everything amusing, including Beatrice.

'Well, it comes to something when wrestling fans watch an elderly woman stall her wheelchair, and think it's part of the act.'

'Elderly?' said Beatrice.

'And I've had enough!'

Mad Brady spluttered on his Kronenberg. 'What? It's in your blood man, from the day you did your first fall.'

'Who you calling elderly?' said Beatrice.

'Well, it's not in my blood now, wrestling's gone mad and I want out!

'I've a few years yet,' muttered Beatrice, 'before I get kicked off to some old folks home.'

Sheryl was about to say something; about to find out which old folks home Beatrice was talking about when Johnston walked into the room, and the crowds parted. He had a presence and he was big, with the sort of smile that paid for his dentist's yearly holiday in the Bahamas. He wore black leather trousers and a Hawaiian shirt, unbuttoned to the waist, showing of the sort of sculptured chest Sheryl would never tire of licking. She watched his beautiful brown body walk towards her, and she forgot all about the Crickey brothers.

Mad Brady and Frank, however, looked surprised.

'Where's the other half?' whispered Frank.

'She's miffed bout the panda, says it stole Johnston's thunder. She's been giving anyone who will listen an earful.' Mad Brady nodded towards Harry. 'Especially him.'

'Water off a duck's back, huh!'

Sheryl watched Johnston cut through the crowd. He looked better than she remembered, leaner, darker and, God, so smooth. She sucked her stomach in harder and cursed the fact that there was no vodka in her coke. For six months, she had privately drooled over Johnston, while all he knew about her was her crap choice of knickers. What the hell was she going to say to him?

'Over here,' waved Mad Brady.

Sheryl's heart pounded as Johnston got closer. She tried to look cool and relaxed.

'Thanks,' said Johnston, holding out a hand the size of a dinner plate, 'for you help today.'

Beatrice grasped 'the dinner plate' and flashed her best smile.

'You like wrestling?' he said in a rich voice.

Sheryl watched Johnston. He had a smile that could melt ice, and a jawline you could run your tongue along. She sighed.

'Oooh yes!' said Beatrice.

'Maybe I could teach you a few moves?'

'Oooh yes!'

Johnston let out a rich chuckle, grasped Sheryl's hand and then looked into her eyes. 'Where's the guy who was with you? I wanted to thank him as well.'

****

Conway stood in the staff ladies toilets. Helen was at the back adjusting his bra, while her friend Jessie was busy stuffing socks down the front.

Conway was almost enjoying himself; it had been a long time since he had the attention of a female that didn't involve the expression of a snarling cat. He looked in the mirror, and wondered about dieting and which loo should he use.

'Orange or red lipstick?' they giggled.

He placed a red wig on his head and practised a playful toss as he had seen in the shampoo ads. Now he knew why his wife always took so long to dress up for their annual Christmas party, it was probably the most fun she had all year. He let Jessie dab a bit of perfume behind his ear, sucked in his breath and looked side on in the mirror, just like he had seen his wife do.

He almost smiled.

****

Nefertiti had no time to meet wrestlers, she was in the dressing room trying to psych herself up for dancing, but somehow her heart wasn't in it. She had lost any desire to be seen or admired, she had, so she told herself, lost the will to dance. She pulled out her padded sequinned bra and sighed. Rodger wasn't there and it just wasn't the same.

She decided a drink was needed if she was to face these people. She picked up her dancing cane, her veil and her cds and headed for the lounge of the Columbia. *A couple of Jack Daniel's,* she thought, *and I'll be fine.*

****

Nefertiti took a seat at the bar and ordered a double. In two gulps, her glass was empty and she was looking at herself in the mirror behind the optics. For the first time, Nefertiti saw an old woman, an old tart, no less. She looked down at the lonely ice sitting at the bottom of her glass. It had been a long time since she felt like this, and a long time since she had stared into an empty glass and wanted more.

'Give us another!' she said, with a wave of her glass. But Finley the barman never heard. He was up the other end of the bar, watching what was probably the ugliest-looking transvestite he had ever seen approach the bar.

'My name is Karin,' Conway squeaked to a silent bar.

'Well Karin,' Finley finally said, with an 'I've seen everything look'. 'Serve yourself over there.'

****

Just as Conway was making his debut as Karin in the lounge bar, Martin was walking into the Columbia Hotel with Chubby, his little Haystack, and most of the women from the gallery, fuelled by expensive champagne, and rich chocolates. Women who, up till now, thought that certain things in life were gone forever, certain things that thanks to Rodger's paintings were now stirring in their loins.

Martin had plans for a quiet entrance; he had pictured an evening of quiet praise and reassurance to Nefertiti from him, and maybe a few of the women. But the women felt differently.

They wanted to meet the artist. They wanted to get his autograph and touch the hand of the man who painted what was, up to now, a mystery. They wanted to meet Nefertiti, the inspiration, the muse, the woman who dared, and they wanted to chant the Flower of Scotland as loud as possible. But as Martin had explained, they would probably be asked to leave.

'God, I haven't felt like this in years,' said one woman, 'so alive, so vibrant.'

'And so randy,' said another.

They followed Martin in to the lounge bar giggling, some secretly whispering Flower Scotland, and waited for something to happen.

****

'I've lost me Rodger and me mojo,' said Nefertiti to Karin. 'Me reason for dancing.'

Karin put a glass under the Jack Daniel's and tapped it for a measure. His plan was unfolding nicely. It was amazing what a stuffed bra and some lipstick could do.

Karin knew Rodger like the back of his police badge. He had

made a study of the man, and always, his downfall was women. Mr. Brassiere or Rodger, as he now called himself, was an old romantic with a love for flowers and the extravagant life. And Nefertiti was just to his taste; skinny and exotic, standing out in the crowd like a parrot in a flock of seagulls.

'I'll never dance again,' muttered Nefertiti. 'He has ripped me heart out.'

And dramatic, thought Conway.

'He has ripped me heart and the soul of my loins.'

Dramatic as a soap opera, thought Karin, and wherever that dramatic old tart was, old Brassier would not be far away. If only McConical could see him now, mused Karin. In fact, he was pretty sure the whole station would be impressed. Ignoring the two men waving their empty glasses at him, Karin took Nefertiti's glass and filled it. When this was all over, he told himself, he was going to get a proper wig.

****

Harry was beginning to get impatient. Where the hell was Nefertiti? He walked into the dressing room to see what was holding Nefertiti up, and found an empty room with a pile of costumes on the floor, the bathroom light on, and the liquor cabinet opened. He smelt the empty glass, Jack Daniel's, at least she had taste.

Harry had been sceptical about the belly dancing idea from the start, but the Sports for Scotland Committee had insisted. If only they had gone with his suggestion; Mactavish's Accordion trio followed by a little salsa for the younger set. But no, they wanted an eighties band 'Frankie spins Spandau' to be precise.

'Have you ever seen this band?' Harry had muttered over the

phone, already knowing the answer. 'A friend of a friend was in the band and they just needed a break,' was the answer. And then Chubby pushed for a belly dancer, Nefertiti to be exact.

'Oh, what a good idea,' said one of the women on the committee. 'It's all the rage in Glasgow, and you have to be fat to do it!'

Now here he was with a reception room full of bored wrestlers and committee members, who would soon be listening to 'Frankie spins Spandou' and waiting for an aging exotic dancer, who by the looks of things, had absconded or at least was pissed.

His reputation as an organiser was not great at the best of times, but this would mean the end of a not particularly great career, and probably him going back to selling men's suits.

Bugger it, thought Harry again, as he headed for the only place left to look; the lounge bar.

****

Sheryl watched a tiny blonde appear from nowhere, wearing tight leathers and a silk shirt unbuttoned low enough to reveal more than one boob job.

'Who's the aging Pamela Anderson?' asked Beatrice.

'Lolita,' said Uno Sumo and Mad Brady in unison. 'Johnston's mother.'

Sheryl looked at her hero, who up till then had been busy trying to talk some waiter into a private wrestling lesson. He didn't look too happy at his mother. In fact, he seemed to shrink as she got closer.

'Harry tells me you're thinking of quitting,' said Lolita, with a playful tap on Frank's leg.

Mad Brady threw Frank a look.

'You'll never quit, you'll be rolling up even when you can't hear and need a piss bag.'

The men laughed uncomfortably, looking about for an escape as Lolita brushed some imaginary crumbs from Johnston shirt. 'You on the tequila already?' she said. Johnston didn't reply, he too was looking for an escape.

Sheryl sipped her diet coke, wishing it was something stronger, something that would blunt the disappointment she now felt. How could the man who hung on her walls, whose perfect body filled her dreams, the Johnston who wrestled like a tiger be the same man who stood before her. The was no witty repartee, no animal magnetism, just some big guy who had stopped drinking tequila cause his mother told him to. She felt almost cheated. She watched Mad Brady and Frank disappear into the crowd. Was it because she was sober that things weren't as great as she planned?

****

Rodger, Steven, and Eric walked into the entrance of the Columbia and stood for a moment collecting their thoughts, Rodger had arranged to meet Martin in the lounge bar.

Steven, under the influence of half a dozen Babychams, was thinking about Martin, Sheryl and what Porter would do in his situation. 'He's here somewhere,' he finally said in a loud voice.

'Sh, you want to get thrown out? Just leave it to me,' said Eric. He approached the receptionist while Rodger headed for the lounge bar, hopefully Martin was already there.

****

Sheryl stared out across the room and saw Steel's seven-foot frame striking a pose in a 'Simply the Best' tee shirt and jeans. He waved to an uncomfortable-looking Johnston and moved towards him.

'Hey Johnston, how'd she take it?'

'Haven't said anything yet, waiting for the…'

'Right time. Yeah, I know. Look, Johnston, you pussy whipped or what? She's your mother, for fuck's sake.'

Johnston looked tired.

'When you decide to take your balls out your mother's purse, just let me know.'

'Let him know what?' said Lolita.

Johnston looked at his empty glass.

Harry, who was standing nearby, was a man who liked to help, a man who was fond of Johnston and had a particular dislike for women of Lolita's calibre. He decided to do the only decent thing possible.

'Fancy a dance,' he said, as Frankie spins Spanduo had just started their Madonna set.

Lolita looked at Harry's soft eyes. She quite liked Vogue, in fact, she probably could remember some of the moves.

'Come on,' said Harry 'let's show 'em how to get down.'

Lolita took his hand and with an 'I'll be back glare' at Johnston, she headed for the dance floor.

Johnston slid his roll-ups back into his pocket and took a chance. Mumbling something about fresh air, he headed for the entrance of the hotel. *A few secret smokes,* he thought, *and I'll feel better and I can face what I have to do.* Then he caught sight of Steven's sweet arse and changed his plans.

Steven was still thinking about Martin, Sheryl and what Porter would do in his situation when he felt a hot breath on the back of his neck, followed by a tap on his shoulder. He jumped then turned to find Johnston standing a little too close for comfort.

'Thanks for your help today,' murmured Johnston.

'Oh I ...it was nothing.'

'You like wrestling?' smiled Johnston.

'No I...'

'I do!' said the receptionist.

'I could teach you a few moves, I could show you how to fall,' said Johnston.

'Er, no, I'm not the athletic type,' said Steven.

'Neither was I,' he said. 'But look at me now.' Johnston pulled up his shirtsleeve and flexed his muscle.

'OOH,' said another woman.

'I'm here to sort things out,' blurted Steven. *And to do what Porter would do,* thought Steven, *if I could just figure out what that is.* Steven swayed a little.

'He's looking for Sheryl,' said Eric.

Johnston had no intentions of showing Steven where Sheryl was. He wanted Steven all to himself. He had dreams and ideas all running through his head, and with one look in Steven's kind eyes, he knew he had found someone who could help, or at least listen.

He sent Eric to the Oyster bar (in search of Sheryl), and led Steven to Nefertiti's changing room, he had something to show Steven.

CHAPTER TWENTY-TWO

Harry walked into the lounge bar and saw Nefertiti miserably trying to give make-up advice to Karin. Harry looked at Nefertiti swaying and Karin in an orange wig and lipstick red enough to stop traffic and wondered about miracles.

Nefertiti looked at Harry. 'I can't dance I'm done for.'

Harry ordered a diet coke. 'What do you mean, done for?'

'Look at me, I used to have a reputation for being gorgeous and yet unavailable, now everyone has seen me Flower of Scotland; in Technicolor.'

'So what am I supposed to do, put on one of your costumes and dance myself?'

'No, but Sheryl could. And she's not looking too bad tonight.'

'She can dance?' spluttered Harry. Maybe that would work, he thought, after all she had a nice smile. Harry, a man of action, downed his diet coke, brought a double for Nefertiti and one for 'Karin' on tap, and headed back up to the Oyster bar, maybe something could be saved.

Nefertiti was busy drinking and thinking and didn't see Martin, Chubby, Imogene and the group of women enter the bar. It was only when Chubby shouted, 'There she is!' that Nefertiti looked up and saw their reflection in the mirror behind the optics.

'Who?' said one of the women.

'Nefertiti.'

'My Nefertiti,' said Rodger standing at the door.

'And Mine,' said Imogene.

181

Karin saw Rodger, and for the first time in years, smiled a complete full-on smile. It had been years since Karin had seen Rodger, and to Karin's mind, he had not aged so well.

Nefertiti, who had no idea about Imogene's change of heart, turned around to see Martin and Imogene smiling at her. *What are they playing at?* she thought. *A smile from a stuck-up cow, who referred to her art as Middle Eastern pole dancing for the desperate. And a smile from the man whose idea of a joke was to send her letters about her rent increase addressed to Nefertiti, Queen of Loch Fyne?* She looked from one smiling face to another as her tumbling emotions turned into the familiar ball of anger, now fuelled with Jack Daniel's.

Finley, a man of little patience, had been pushed to the limits by the useless barmaid who had done nothing but talk to an aging lush. He pushed a tray of Bacardi Breezers at her, 'Here, for the women who have just come in stinking of Joss sticks.'

Karin pushed them back. 'I've got better things to do.'

****

George hopped out of the taxi like a man twenty years younger than he was, and with a whistle wheeled the chair into the hotel.

'Hi George,' yelled the receptionist.

'Hey G,' yelled a waiter walking past.

George, with a jaunty wave, headed for the Oyster bar. The first thing he saw was a very grim-looking Beatrice sitting in the corner, too embarrassed to move her chair. He gave her a wave and strolled past the bar as Frankie goes to Hollywood played at full pelt.

Relax go to it when you want to suck to it...

Beatrice looked up to see George's sturdy figure cut through the crowd and almost smiled.

182

'What you doing here then?'

when you want to coooooooome…

'I brought another chair for you.'

'I see, your sister's?' said Beatrice, looking unimpressed. 'You'll have to push me then.'

Ah ah aha when you want to cooooome

George smiled, *As predictable as ever*, he thought. He sidled the chair beside Beatrice and motioned her to get in. 'I can take you to a nice quiet place as well if you like.'

'Sheryl's going to dance,' said Beatrice. 'Apparently, the Queen of the Clyde is pissed and refusing to dance.'

'Oh,' said George with a smile; watching Sheryl belly dance had always been a wee fancy of his.

****

Iain and Cocolder were sitting in the office discussing Conway, when Finley pushed opened the door and hobbled in. 'Need your help,' he puffed to the backs of the two men. 'Trouble in the lounge.'

Cocolder placed his coffee back on the saucer and turned to face the whisker-less Finley, 'Not the wrestlers then?' he squeaked.

'No,' said Finley, puffing up his thin chest. 'It's in the bar, some ladies are showing photos of …'

'But we have salsa playing,' said Iain,' Is no one easily pleased any more?'

Cocolder looked at Finley, he didn't particularly like people who only spoke to him when they needed something.

'There's this belly dancing woman drinking Jack Daniel's and …' He took a seat and rubbed his foot. 'I was attacked… with a cane and then these women talking 'bout embracing the sister within, and a guy talking bout his bugle. Then the woman with the cane told him what he could do with his bugle, and then, oh God, they showed the photos again.' Finely shook his head.

Martin had taken photos of the Flower of Scotland exhibition on his mobile, and while Nefertiti was dealing with her big ball of anger, the phone was being passed around.

'They are powerful,' said someone.

'Strong,' said another.

'That's when I put the salsa on like you suggested,' said Finley, with an 'I did my f-ing best' look. 'Rickie Martin no less.'

Iain raised his eyes to the ceiling.

'Then SHE stood up. 'Strong,' SHE says, 'I give 'em bleeding strong,' and began to twirl her cane like this.' Finley began to hobble about like a drunken shot putter with tunnel vision. 'Only thing is, she's been on the piss, and I tried to stop her and got this for my trouble,' said Finley, pointing his foot at the two unimpressed looking men. 'And,' he said, drawing himself up to his full 5'5" height, 'I'll be wantin' compensation.'

Cocolder sighed, tenderly wrapped up his sandwich from his wife and made for the lounge with Iain and Finley, hobbling a respectable distance behind.

****

'I have these ideas,' said Johnston leading Steven into the changing room. Steven looked at the pile of costumes on the floor and for a moment, hoped they weren't anything to do with Johnston.

Johnston poured himself a drink.

'Lolita doesn't know about me and Steel. She keeps trying to pair me off with one of them women wrestlers; frankly, I'd rather pull a pint than one of those girls. You want some?' said Johnston, gesturing with a bottle of tequila.

Steven shook his head. He was starting to sober up and had vague memories of waffling on about Porter.

'Maybe you should try something different to this Sheryl. What about Porter?

'Porter is a character in my book...'

'Your book; I knew you were an artist. I bet you there is another Steven in there bursting to get out. And I bet I could find something to fire that pretty little imagination of yours.'

Steven stopped at the word pretty. Did he just call him pretty? He watched as Johnston walked into the bathroom. 'You know, you're the first person I've met who isn't bothered about the fame thing or my body, I'm more than a body, you know. I have a brain and ideas,'

'Ideas?'

'And Steel wants to get involved.'

Steven was starting to feel a little uncomfortable. Through the door, he could hear the odd rip of clothing... and then a few grunts... what the hell was he doing in there?

Steven scribbled out a note.

Dear Johnston.

(And then crossed out the dear and put TO instead.)

Perhaps you should grab the bull by the horns and tell your mother...

'You see, Steven; we are kindred spirits. I knew that from the moment you rolled me onto my back, from the touch of your hands...'

'That was Sheryl,' said Steven, scribbling out bull and horns.

'I want to create a place where artists like me go and feel safe. See those costumes on the floor. They're mine ...'

I knew it, thought Steven.

'You still there?'

'Well actually, I was just thinking of leaving. I really must find Sheryl and ...'

'Let me show you my plan.'

The bathroom door clicked open and Johnston filled the doorway.

'What do you think?' he said.

His large body wavered just slightly as he casually leant against the doorframe, with one hand resting on his hip. His dark body was bare but for a pink corset and stockings, knee-high boots and a fluorescent G-string stretched to full capacity. His padded bosom heaved with each breath.

Bloody hell, thought Steven.

Johnston wiggled his pelvis, causing a flutter of glitter, 'Cool huh? I made it myself. I'm going into business with Steel, feminine clothes for the larger man, it's all in the cut,' said Johnston. 'And the material, this is stretch see, and Velcro, lots of Velcro. Just think, all those big men who can't get a thing to wear and look at these boots ...cool huh?'

Steven knelt beside Johnston to feel his boots, just as Sheryl and Harry walked into the room.

'Ah,' slurred Johnston, 'the wobbly belly dancer.'

****

Sheryl and Harry surveyed the scene, and in silence came to the same conclusion.

'What the hell are you doing, Johnston, that guy is as straight as a flag pole...' said Harry.

'I know, but he's an artist like me. He understands the creative process.'

'That creative process is going to get its arse kicked if you don't tell your mother soon, Steel ain't that patient.'

'My mother has no idea of the word listen,' said Johnston. 'I got to get her in the right mood.'

'If she is anything like mine, there isn't a right mood,' said Sheryl. 'Nightmare on wheels, that's my mum; she's the sort of woman who thinks silence and a stare is communicating, and a good bra solves everything.'

The three men looked at Sheryl's large chest heaving seductively under the velvet corset.

'In your case, honey,' said Harry 'it works wonders.'

'All's I want,' said Johnston, 'is my own shop with soft lighting and real coffee with those little chocolate covered coca beans on the saucers, and armchairs with matching cushions, and changing rooms, God, decent changing rooms...'

'Yeah, yeah, I know, just tell your fucking mother, Johnston.'

Sheryl watched her hero pout, and she wondered more and more about a drink as she began to realise that there was now no fantasy to get her through the day, no poster on her wall that would make her feel better, and no point to watching wrestling any more.

****

Cocolder, with great presence, made his way to the lounge bar and walked in on Rickie Martin's *Living La Vida Loca* playing in the background, and Nefertiti trying to hold her own. She was twirling her cane about her head and speaking in a restrained angry voice that was quickly losing control. And no one seemed to be bothered. In fact, most of the women were watching Nefertiti like she was some sort of

Goddess, and her cane twirling had some sort of mystical quality to it, as well as being in time to Rickie Martin.

'That woman is ready to blow,' whispered Cocolder to Iain. 'We need to go canny.'

She'll make you live her crazy life

Or she'll take away your pain

Like a bullet to your brain

Canny, thought Iain, *that woman is swinging her cane dangerously near not only to my chandelier, but my customers, and no one's bothered?*

'You have shown us the way,' said Imogene, with a serene smile.

'Way to where,' said Nefertiti, letting her cane drop a little.

'Self-respect; women need someone like you; someone who's not afraid of who she is, even if others do laugh.'

Upside inside out

Living La Vida Loca

Now Nefertiti was really confused, she let her cane fall to her side. 'Who's laughin'?' she finally said.

'Someone your age trying to be sexy,' said Imogene, 'everyone thought it was funny.'

'Funny? Sexy?'

'Those paintings capture the true Nefertiti,' said Rodger.

'Yes, yes totally,' muttered some while others nodded.

'My fanny is funny?' said Nefertiti.

'No!' said Martin, 'Just look at these pictures.'

He passed the phone across to Nefertiti. She looked at the pictures and saw what Rodger saw, and for the first time in a long time, let him move close to her.

Karin watched; Rodger's guard was down; this was his moment, he snuck up behind Nefertiti.

With each picture Nefertiti looked at, she felt closer to her Rodger, and the burden of the last few months rolled away. By the time she got to the end, she felt inspired by the Flower of Scotland collection, inspired by *La Vida Loca* still playing, and more than a little inspired by the half bottle of Jack Daniel's. She tilted her head to the stars; the same stars that shine over the sands of Egypt, and let out a shrill howl from the bottom of her lungs. She then lifted her cane (to the same stars) and began to twirl it in time to the music, this time dancing for pleasure. For this was going to be her last dance. There was a new Nefertiti, she thought, a new path to follow, a path Rodger had seen long before she had...

Karin was taken by surprise and never had a chance.

By the time Cocolder was at the bar, Karin's head had already made contact with Nefertiti's cane, and by the time Cocolder had parted the crowds around Nefertiti, Karin was falling against the wall, and Cocolder along with everyone else could only watch as Karin slid in slow motion down the wall like an egg on a windscreen. His wig caught on a nail and hung there like a red spider, not sure which way to go as his head continued to slide down the wall.

The heels of his shoes skidded along the polished floor, and as his legs parted, his skirt hoisted up revealing very hairy bits of his body, which no amount of nylon could disguise.

Living the La Vida Loca

Living the La Vida Loca

Living the la Vida Loca

There were a few 'Oh my God' shouts from the crowd as his head finally thumped onto the floor, with the disco lights flashing on his bald patch in time to the music.

La la la la la la LA!

La la la la la la LA!

'And I was going to give him a makeup lesson,' muttered Nefertiti.

****

Cocolder stepped into the centre as the music stopped. He took one look at the unconscious Karin and nearly choked on his cheese and pickle. It was that bastard on the fax machine, he thought and threw Iain an 'it's in the bag' look. Cocolder rolled up his sleeves (revealing a large muscular arm) and hoisted the unconscious Conway over his shoulder like a lightweight blanket.

'Ooooh,' said some of the ladies as he walked by.

'On yer self,' muttered a few of the locals.

Cocolder strode in silence through the parted crowd. *My work here is done,* he thought, and didn't even hear as Finley yelled, 'But what about her…with the stick.'

****

Sheryl was in the bathroom standing in front of the mirror while Johnston was zipping up her costume.

Twenty minutes ago, Johnston had been telling Sheryl all about his plans, and showing her some of his work when Beatrice was wheeled in by George, carrying Sheryl's costume.

'You'll be needing this,' she said, dumping the dress on Sheryl's lap.

Sheryl said nothing, she was stunned. Her mother was full of surprises, and bringing her costume was certainly one of them; but with George wheeling her about and the two of them looking like a couple, that was even more bizarre.

'My mum must be getting soft in her old age,' muttered Sheryl. While Johnston unravelled the costume, 'Oh my god,' he said. 'Do you do these in extra large?'

Johnston helped Sheryl get changed, offered her some of his glitter and even let her use some of his body tape.

'The grey knicker lady is gone forever,' he said, looking at her reflection, just as Steven walked in. It was the first time Steven had ever seen Sheryl in her costume, and he was even more impressed than Johnston.

Sheryl caught the look on his face and blushed.

'You look great,' said Steven.

'She looks the business,' Harry said, with a thumbs up at Sheryl. Harry was on his mobile talking to Mohammad about playing his drums. He had been for the last twenty minutes; he had a feeling in his waters that this was his chance to turn things around and resurrect his reputation as an organiser. If Sheryl was as good as Nefertiti said, then all she needed was the right build up and the right audience. He put his hand over the phone and whispered to Sheryl, 'I'm going to give you an entrance that costume deserves.'

'Oh,' said Sheryl. She was beginning to feel a little scared. The last thing she wanted to do was ruin the only decent fantasy she had left; that she was worth watching, that she could rustle up a routine of shimmies that could hold an audience for the length of a song. If she destroyed this last fantasy, what then?

She was still staring at the mirror when a caustic-looking Beatrice wheeled herself back in, 'Hurry up, Sheryl. Eric's taken over with his karaoke.'

'Do you think I can do it?' said Sheryl.

'You'll be great,' said Steven.

'And I'll be cheering for you...' said Beatrice, 'even if no one else does.'

'Thanks Mum.'

'And it will be over before you know it, then we can go back to normality,' said Beatrice.

'But I don't want normality,' said Sheryl.

Beatrice snorted as George walked in with an 'I've been looking for you everywhere' look. 'Come on, let's get you out of here,' he said. And to Sheryl's surprise, Beatrice didn't argue.

'And by the way,' yelled Beatrice from the passage. 'Martin and Imogene are there with old Nef, but don't worry I think they're pissed.

This time, Sheryl snorted, *I'll show her*, she thought.

****

George pushed Beatrice into the Oyster Bar, 'Could you not have said she looked nice?' he said.

'Nice? She don't look nice, she looks fantastic. Now, come on, let's find a place where she can't see me, don't want to put her off.'

'Haven't you just done that already?'

'On the contrary, my dear Watson, sometimes a little anger is needed.'

****

Sheryl stood at the doorway. Harry had arranged a big build up with Mohammad and his drums. He cleared the dance floor and instructed Sheryl to 'make 'em wait.' Sheryl's chest pounded with mixed emotions as she waited for the nod from Steven. When it finally came, Sheryl, with a veil wrapped around her costume and an 'Eat you words, Mother' strut burst in to the bar.

The music was powerful and the women started to clap as Sheryl circled her hips. Then as the tempo changed to slow rhythms, Sheryl slowed her pace and began to unwrap her veil, teasing the audience with a glimpse of her costume.

Sheryl moved from stomach rolls to hip circles and flicks, and then pelvic tilts, her body rippling like jelly. Steven watched, she was just as he imagined her to be; voluptuous, strong and happy.

Under the instigation of Harry, Sheryl stood on to the bar, and let her veil simmer to the ground, revealing her costume. Mohammad let rip on the tabla and with Ardenne's words in her head, Sheryl let the drums unleash the woman in her, catching each beat with her hips.

Then just to add a bit of panache, she picked up a jug and began to balance it on her head, easing herself down onto the floor with mesmerizing movement.

'She dances like an Egyptian,' said Mohammad.

'Like a real pro,' yelled Mad Brady.

'Like an artist,' said Nefertiti, who was sitting very close to her Rodger.

'That's my girl,' muttered Beatrice.

Sheryl worked the floor, seductively twisting her leg to the slow rhythm of the drums, still balancing the jug. She looked into the dark and saw Beatrice with George by her side, looking proud, a look Sheryl had not seen for years.

As the music built up tempo, Sheryl stood up from the floor and quickened her step.

Now her hips moved without her thinking. She felt an exhilaration never experienced before. She looked around the audience, and they were all clapping, some even cheering. Sheryl felt a huge surge of happiness; she ditched the jug and began to circle to the music. She started to think about Nefertiti's new plans, and all that had happened in the last few days. She started to think of Steven and his offers of help, she looked at him clapping his heart out, and felt a plan forming, an idea of how to make a life for herself and maybe earn a living that didn't involve a Hoover.

CHAPTER TWENTY-THREE

Conway woke in a hospital bed with a thumping head and a blurry vision.

A nurse looked pityingly at him, 'Do you remember who you are yet, luv?'

Conway thought of Cocolder, his wife and the station.

'No, I don't think I do,' he said, with a serene look on his face. Conway focused on the nurse's sweet face, she had blond hair tied in a bun and pink lipstick, he looked across at his red wig slumped on the bedside cabinet and decided that blond was more his colour.

CHAPTER TWENTY-FOUR

Sheryl drove into the garage in her new van with
'SHERYL'S DIY NO JOB TOO SMALL'
written on the side.

It had been a busy day for Sheryl. Steven had booked four jobs for her. Steven took most of her bookings for DIY. Steven had put a poster in the library and one in the community centre (where he now taught creative writing), and it wasn't long before Sheryl was busy enough to buy a van.

Sheryl jumped out of the van and ran into her flat above the garage, slipped a Hossam Ramsey CD on and jumped into the shower. Steven, along with Imogene and Chubby, were picking her up in twenty minutes.

It was a two-hour drive to Glasgow, and the plan was to meet the rest of the Sisterhood at the Buchannan St Bus Station. The Sisterhood had been practising for months, this was to be their first BIG gig.

Steven had the journey all planned, with freshly ground coffee in flasks, herby baguettes filled with salad and cheese, and some yoghurt to follow.

'Something light,' he said 'before the performance.'

Imogene called it spiritual food for the sisters.

While Chubby, who was tiring of the whole Sisterhood thing and was thinking of going back to Rugby, called it a bloody baguette and insisted on stopping for a roll and sausage.

****

George pulled the covers up over Beatrice, switched on the TV and poured them both a Royal Bracklier. 'I like living in sin!' he said.

Beatrice said nothing, being content was not something she liked to talk about. He put the dram by her bedside and tuned the TV to The Art Stops Here show.

****

Judge Dougie, the host, was standing outside the Buchanan Galleries talking to Johnston about his new boutique, and the Flower of Scotland Exhibition held in the Buchanan Galleries.

'So, you're opening a shop in Glasgow?'

'That's right, JD, a shop for men who are looking for something a little different.'

'Like what you're wearing?'

'Yes Sir, you like?'

'Do we like?' yelled JD, revving up the crowd. The crowd cheered and clapped as Johnston did a jaunty turn in his outfit.

'My boy's always been different,' said Lolita, brushing imaginary fluff from her son's back. 'My boy's an artist.'

****

'And making a bucket,' said Beatrice.

****

Harry stood at the top floor of the Buchanan Galleries, talking to a drama student sitting in a panda suit, who was wondering what a panda had to do with abstract fannies.

'I want you to wear this during your routine, it's one of Johnston's creations.'

The student looked at the jewelled cod piece and sighed, *The things you did for your equity card,* he thought.

'And I want you to do this,' Harry said, illustrating star shapes with his chubby legs. 'And this, and maybe this…'

'Alright, I get the picture,' muttered the student.

Harry pulled a card from his jacket, which no longer was the creased, size-to-small variety, but the tailor-made slimming variety, and handed the card to the student.

Harry and Martin Promotions LTD

Thanks to Sheryl, he and Martin had moved on to bigger things. Johnston products for the womanly men; The Unveiling of the Flower of Scotland; The Chronicles of Nefertiti, and The Sisterhood (although he still wanted to work on their name).

The student slipped the card into his pocket, slipped on the codpiece and adjusted his harness. *I'm on TV,* he told himself, *that's all that matters.*

****

Johnston was still talking to JD when the drumming started. Ten men in kilts and bare, oiled chests walked through the crowd drumming. For the first time in years, Lolita was too busy watching to speak.

Once the drummers were lined along the edge of the carpet, the Sisterhood began to emerge from the crowd with their capes trailing on the wet ground. They formed a circle on the red carpet and after an impressive routine, dropped their capes and hit the ground, revealing Sheryl in the middle, striking a pose.

****

'Impressive,' said George.

'Bit over the top for an artist who only last year was painting murals for the postie.'

George, with a tuneless whistle, sauntered to the bathroom, 'I've a wee surprised for you, Bea, so go easy on the whisky.'

'Don't like surprises.'

George laughed as he shut the bathroom door, 'Oh, I think you'll like this one!'

****

Martin sat with Nefertiti and Rodger, who were in the limousine. It stopped at the bottom of the red carpet and as they got out, Martin lent over to the driver and handed him a card.

Martin and Harry Promotions LTD

The crowd applauded as Rodger, dressed in green with trimmed sideboards, stepped out and, with great ceremony, held the door open for Nefertiti.

'And here's herself,' said JD. 'Wearing the biggest greenest sequined turban I've ever seen. What do you think of that, Johnston?'

'Nefertiti,' chanted the crowd.

Two scantily-clad young men followed behind as they walked down the red carpet.

'I like that,' said Johnston.

'Nefertiti, Nefertiti!'

Nefertiti stretched out her arms as the scantily-clad men took her cloak, then she closed her eyes and titled her head back as if praying to the sky.

'Nefertiti, over here!'

She took a microphone off JD.

'HELLO Glasgow,' she said.

'NEFERTITI, NEFERTITI!' The crowd began to clap.

Nefertiti held her hand up, silencing the crowd.

'This is art at its finest, and womanhood as it should be!'

****

Beatrice emptied her glass. 'Dramatic as fuck.'

'You ready, Beatrice,' shouted George from the bathroom.

Beatrice looked at the TV as the panda started his descent to the Proclaimers and sighed, 'Anything's better than this.'

With a small fanfare, George opened the door and causally leaned against the doorframe with nothing on but a codpiece. He swung it in time to the Proclaimers.

When you gooo, will ye send back a letter from America.

Beatrice laughed so hard she nearly fell off the bed.

'With compliments from Rodger,' said George, and with a jaunty swagger, made his way slowly to her bed.

****

At the end of a very successful evening, Steven and Sheryl stood watching Nefertiti air kiss an unknown MP.

'You driving,' she said, 'or me?'

Steven lifted an M&S carrier bag and looked into her sweet blue eyes. 'My pal has left me the key to his flat for the night, Eggs Benedict, Columbian coffee and some fresh oranges.'

Sheryl smiled, 'Sounds good to me.'

Steven took her down Buchanan street, and as they walked close to each other, Steven looked at the drizzle just beginning to splash on the pavement and smiled, as Porter would say, life is all about timing.